COME BACK WITH ME

A story of one man's life and his dedication to spreading the Word.

STEVEN J MATHEWS

Published by Purple Parrot Publishing

Printed in the United Kingdom

First Printing, 2021

ISBN: Print: 978-1-8383723-8-5

Purple Parrot Publishing

www.purpleparrotpublishing.co.uk

Edited by Viv Ainslie

Follow Steven at:

https://www.facebook.com/stevenjmathewsauthor/

ACKNOWLEDGEMENTS

Thank you to my parents, who made me.

Thank you to my wife, who made me.

Thank you to my children, who made me.

Thank you to Vivienne, who made me.

Steven J Mathews

CONTENTS

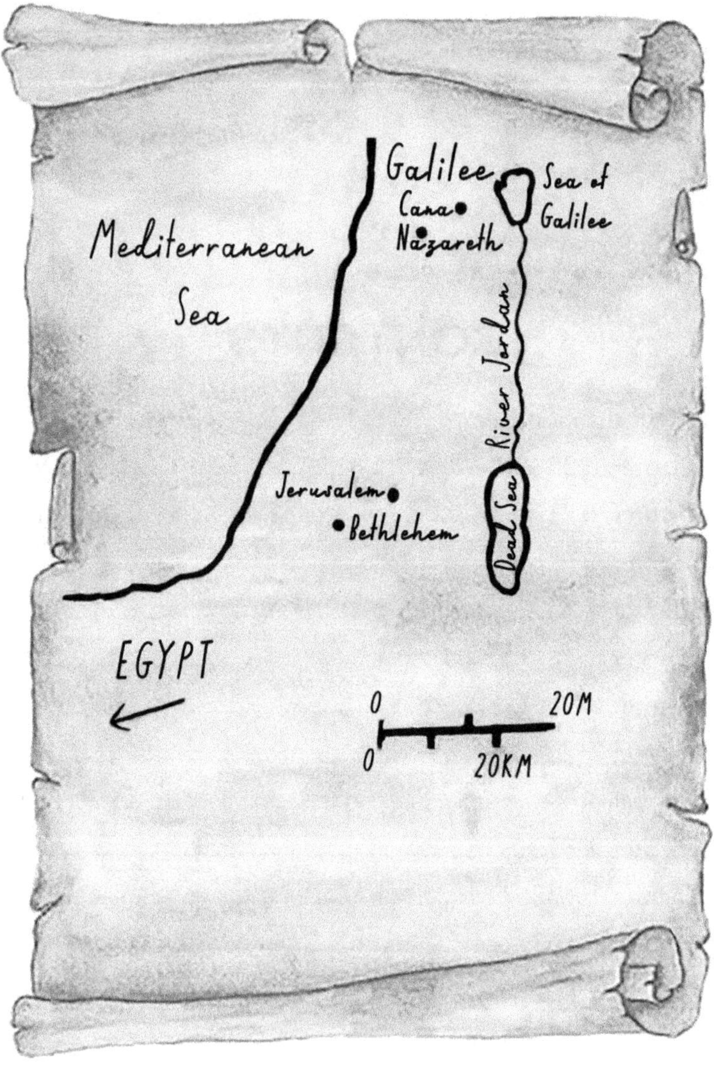

Galilee

Cana

Nazareth

Sea of
Galilee

Mediterranean

Sea

River Jordan

Jerusalem

Bethlehem

Dead Sea

EGYPT

0   20M

0   20KM

ABOUT THIS BOOK

I was lucky enough to go on a trip to the Holy Land and visit many of the places mentioned in the Bible. Having listened to the stories of these places and at school and church, suddenly were no longer stories but real events which I can now relate to.

This is not a rewrite of the Bible, although I have used it as a reference. It's a story about the life and times of Jesus as he grew and travelled. I have used many characters familiar to us all from the gospels and loosely based my storylines on well-known stories. These are all told by Jesus himself. He is telling you the story of his life as it unfolds before him. I didn't want this to be a biblical travel brochure or a "and then we went..." story.

The chapters are in relevance to his age (with his age below the chapter title). As little is known about the early years, this makes some chapters less full than later ones. I have used my imagination and a little bit of fact.

Steven

CHAPTER 1

33

I can barely open my right eye. Pain now immense.

But through this eye, I can see the faces staring in disbelief.

"Forgive them Lord for they know not what they do!"

My words fall on deaf ears. My throat is dry and just a crackle of sound comes out. I know I must endure this spectacle. I must be brave. I must not take it personally.

"I do this for you… the people… the future. But the pain; please make it quick Lord."

My mind is starting to wander. Wander through the years and I feel myself drifting into the past… drifting slowly – like a stream trickling backwards.

Back…

Back…

Back.

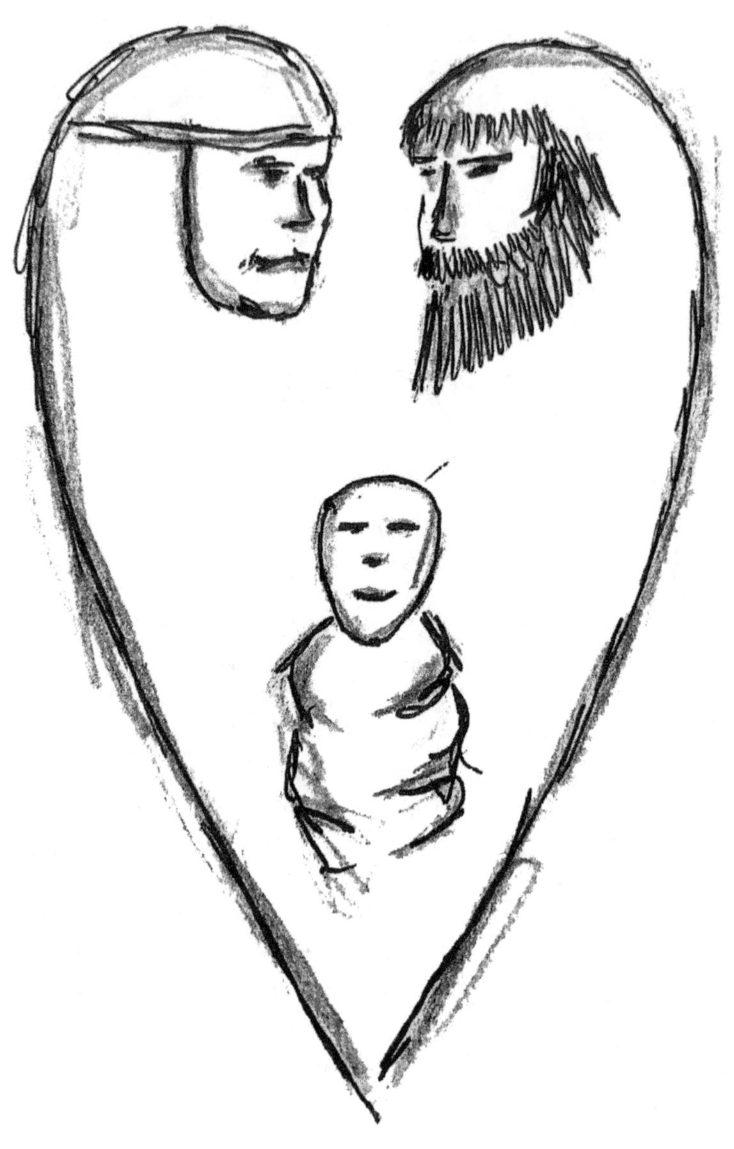

CHAPTER 2

2

"Mamma, Mamma."

"Joseph, Joseph. Come quickly. Listen… He's just spoken his first words."

Mother's face lit up at the fact that I said 'Mamma' first! Father came scurrying in dishevelled then looked on smiling in contentment.

"I have to finish these chairs today ready for the market if you want food on the table for him."

My father is a patient man and gladly gives in to Mother's excitable nature but he has a more practical approach to life. He had hand-built our modest mud-brick house with an area for cooking and living, and an area for sleeping. The furniture was all handmade by him too, even the crib which I, his baby son, lay smiling and gurgling in. He was very highly regarded in his profession as a carpenter.

I was born in Bethlehem. My mother and father had to go there for a census that was being carried out by a Roman Governor called Quirinius. He wanted to calculate the number of people who lived in our land so everyone had to go back to the place of their birth.

So, my mother riding on a donkey, heavily pregnant with me, and my father travelled to Bethlehem to register. When they arrived, the place was so busy – there were so many other people and there was nowhere to stay. An innkeeper, seeing my mother was heavily pregnant, took pity and offered them a place in a stable at the back of his inn where he kept a cow, a goat and two sheep. It was dry and clean with fresh straw. This is where I was born.

My mother often told me a story about some men who came to visit us at that place soon after I was born. They came bearing gifts and though my parents were happy to receive visitors, they were confused why these men had come. They were wise men, some called them Magi, and they said they had travelled a long way because they believed a prophecy had been fulfilled by me being born under a special star.

Mother and Father didn't talk about this event until the day news came that King Herod had murdered his own family one by one. His mind was troubled and he believed his family was conspiring against him. Then he was given news of a prophecy of the coming of a new Messiah – a newborn child – and his already troubled mind spiralled out of control. He sent word out around the lands that all newborn boys, up to the age of two, were to be killed. Troops of Herod's soldiers were sent out to find and kill all the newborn boys.

One day, my father had gone into the village for supplies and there was something happening. He asked a group of people what was wrong but they all spoke at once and he couldn't understand them. A little old lady grabbed Father's arm and told him about Herod's intentions and that if we loved our son, we should leave and go somewhere far away. He was so moved by the old lady's words that he rushed home straight away.

He ran through the doorway and called out, "Mary. Mary."

She was at the fire baking some bread and turned around, startled by my father's panicked entrance.

"What on earth is it, Joseph?"

Father told her what was going on, that they had to leave straight away because I was in danger. They were going to go to Egypt where it was safe and far away from Herod's rule.

They gathered their belongings and packed them onto the donkey, tied the goats with twine and secured them to the donkey's saddle. They needed to be on the road as the sun would be high, making it too hot to travel. Mother took one last look around and blessed the little house. She truly hoped to return to her home one day.

Without looking back, we started on the road to Egypt. It was to be a long, arduous journey across the desert. With many bandits and robbers, it was no place for a young family but we pushed on. Sometimes there was hard ground although mostly it was soft sand and this made walking with the animal's hard work. Our poor donkey was laden beyond his means. It had to be done as we were going to camp under the stars for at least four nights and our first night was fast approaching.

That first night the sun sank very quickly and you could feel the chill of the night approach. We stopped and Father made a fire while Mother unpacked the tent. This was how each of these nights went.

We made it safely to Egypt. There were a lucky few who escaped the terrible fate Herod was inflicting on his people. I was one of those. God must have been looking out for me.

I was still only two when we moved to Egypt and had no idea what was happening. It was all a great adventure to me.

I often thought about that story of the Wise men and the prophecy they spoke of as I grew up, but it became less of reality and more of a story to tell by the fireside. I never understood it; until now.

Egypt was a fabulous place – it seemed so much more advanced than Judea. Where we had small mud-brick houses and tents in Judea, the Egyptians had built huge pointed structures for their leader to be buried in after they died. They called them pyramids. Most people lived in large buildings with many levels shared with other families above and beside each other. They worshipped many gods and carved their images out of large stones which were placed all around. Father would take me to show me these wonders and he would try to work out how they had made them but he was a carpenter, not a stonemason. He got a bit frustrated trying to work out how these icons and the pyramids were created.

Mother would take me to the market and we would see all sorts of bright coloured things that people had made. I noticed that they painted around their eyes with a black paint called kohl. Not only the women but the men too and some added red colour to their cheeks. I asked Father why they did this and he just replied, "The Egyptians are a different culture to us and this is their way." I just accepted that.

I started to make a few friends but we couldn't talk much as I was only just getting to grips with my own language let alone speaking another. Nevertheless, I still played with some of the other children and we managed to communicate even though it was rudimentary – lots of hand signals. By the age of five, I had picked up more and more words. I tried to tell them about my God and how wonderful he was but they couldn't understand that I had only one god where they had many. So, who was right and who was wrong? I was too young to understand any of it. As long as all were happy it didn't seem to matter and I accepted their way – I was living in their land after all.

As Egyptian religions and beliefs were different to my family's, there were no temples or synagogues to worship in. Instead, we gave our thanks and prayers at home. Nobody minded and we were accepted into the local community but kept ourselves to ourselves. Father thought it best that way with the troubles that we had left behind. Herod had no power in Egypt, so we felt safe, for now. The ruler here, called the Pharaoh, was believed to be a living god. Pharoah believed he was a god and all his people worshipped him. So, not only did they have gods for everything, they had a Pharoah who was also a god they had to worship. It was all very confusing for my young brain.

We stayed in Egypt until Herod died and the troubles were over. Father wanted to go back to Bethlehem but the new ruler, Herod's son, also called Herod, was no better than his father. It was decided that we should start a new life in Galilee. Mother said it would be nice to live by the sea. Once again, we packed up and made our way to Galilee and our new future.

CHAPTER 3

8

The years passed slowly, as they do when you're young. I helped my father with the animals and he taught me how to use his wonderful tools. "Put that down," would be his favourite saying. "You'll hurt yourself – it's sharp." But I never listened, I was too eager to learn. Well, I was eight!

Sometimes I would wander off into the village where I'd sit listening to the sermons and talking with the elders about all sorts of wonderful stories. Then my mother would come running in and scoop me up.

"What have I told you about wandering off?" she would say in her overprotective voice.

"Don't worry Mother," I'd say calmly, "no harm can come to me in my Father's house."

She would look at me with such love, kiss my forehead and lead me off by my ear.

Our town was a nice, neat little place called Nazareth in Galilee. As I grew, I became friendly with most of its inhabitants. There were the usual things you find in a town. There was a bakery owned by a big, jolly man called Simeon and a fish stall which, on a really hot day, you couldn't pass without putting your hand over your nose. The owner, an older man called Jacob, always smelled the same as his stall and no one could stand near him for long.

There was also an old lady selling lemons. Her face and hands were very wrinkly and she walked stooped to one side. I called her Nana and she always smiled at me when I called her that. We would sit and chat for ages and she never complained about her ailments; she just said, "It's God's will."

One day I went to town to see Nana and she wasn't there. I asked Simeon the baker where she was and he told me, "She has gone home as she has not been well."

I ran as fast as my bare feet could go to Nana's house and her door was shut. Without thinking, I pushed my way in calling softly, "Nana… Nana."

I found her lying on her bed of straw. She looked up at me with her toothless smile and held out her shaking hand, "Come boy, sit, sit," she said, coughing painfully. I hesitated but slowly knelt beside her and took her hand.

"How can I help?" I pleaded.

"You're a good boy and we have become good friends. But now I must go on a wonderful journey."

Puzzled, I looked at her. She gave a short gasp and as a tear fell from her glazed eyes, she lay quietly back and stared with blank eyes at the ceiling.

"Nana," I whispered. "Nana."

But she was gone. I held her hand which felt strangely smooth. My eyes filled with tears – this was the first friend who had died. Death had taken her. That unforgiving word *death*.

I put her hand on her chest and seemed to remember the elders saying words of comfort to other families who had lost a loved one, so I put my hands together in prayer.

"Ha'makom yenahem etkhem betokh she'ar avelei Tziyonvi'Yerushalayim." This means, "May God console you among the other mourners of Zion and Jerusalem." I didn't know what else to say but I felt right saying it.

I ran all the way home without stopping, went into the house and lay on the bed sobbing. Mother came in, "What on Earth is wrong my son!" she asked while cradling my head.

"It's Nana," I sobbed. "She's dead!"

Mother cuddled me into her and explained, "All life comes to an end and when God wants us to go and live with him, we have to obey."

"But why Nana she was kind and she was my friend? I don't understand this."

She looked into my eyes and gave me that all-knowing smile.

"When we are born into this life, we come in at God's

pleasure. Then, there comes a time when he wants us back. Today it was Nana's turn."

Her words rang softly in my ear; for an eight-year-old, it was the best explanation.

"Come," she smiled, "let us have some bread and you can have goat's milk. Then we shall remember Nana in a prayer."

I found it hard to eat the bread at first but as I washed it down with the milk, I found myself coming to terms with it all. Mother knelt, clasped my hands in hers and we began to pay tribute to Nana.

"Remember her as she was. Remember all the good times you spent with her. And when you want her near, remember her face. Now close your eyes and picture her."

I closed my eyes and imagined. There was Nana in front of me as if she had never left. I quickly opened them to see Mother's head bent down; Nana had gone. I realised then that all I had to do was close my eyes and there she would be. This was a great comfort to me.

As an eight-year-old, I had a very carefree and happy life and did all the things an eight-year-old would do. Mother and Father taught me everything about life and it helped me take all its challenges in my stride.

CHAPTER 4

13

Soon it was to be my 13th birthday and I was to go to the place where the elders met. That was when I would become a man.

Most of the elders had time for me as I somehow took in all that they were saying. When I questioned them, they would answer as if I was grown up. I never felt like a child in their presence and they never treated me as such. While all the other boys were off climbing trees and cliffs or chasing goats, I would spend all my spare time with the elders.

Now I was 13. It was time for my bar mitzvah, which was a grand affair with all the people from the village joining in. My cousins James and Simon were also there to become of age. It was a long-drawn-out affair but somehow, I took it all in. James and Simon, on the other hand, were like mice trapped in a cage; not able to stand still or concentrate in any way. I remember one of the elders tapping James on the head with a long stick and it made him still for a few moments but he was soon back jumping around.

After the ceremony, the women laid the tables for everyone to celebrate at and someone started singing and the men started dancing together in a big circle. So, now being a man, I could join in the dance, along with James and Simon. At the end of the song, we all clapped and cheered. The feast went on for hours and it was so warm. Towards the end, I was getting tired so I went outside to where the night air was a little cooler. I wandered over to where Nana used to sit with her basket of lemons and sat myself down on her spot and closed my eyes.

"So, you have become a man today?"

I opened my eyes with a start but there was no one there. I looked around and still no one. Was my mind playing tricks? Did I eat something to make me dream? Once again, I sat back down and closed my eyes.

"Do not be afraid my boy, for it is I, Nana."

Once again, I opened my eyes and sure enough, there she was. I gasped. My mouth opened as if to speak but no words came out.

Eventually, I made managed to blurt out, "Is it really you Nana?"

I couldn't believe my eyes but she was really there. There was something different about her; she seemed more radiant, almost shimmering.

"I have been watching you as you grow and I must say that I'm very pleased with you."

I stared unbelievably still trying to speak again but unable.

"Do not fear my boy. I am your guardian angel and I have always been with you. Whenever your need has been great or your heart and soul weak."

I managed to stand up and noticed that we were the same height; Nana was now straight and true without blemish or mark, yet she was still that wonderful old woman that I had grown to love and know since my early youth.

I reached out to touch her hand but could not find it, it was as if she were air. Yet I did not feel scared; I had a warm, safe feeling which surrounded me.

"Nana," I managed.

"Farewell my little one, it is time for me to go but do not despair for I will always be here."

She pointed to my chest. I looked down. When I looked back up again, she had gone. I sat back down on the floor and put my face into my hands.

What did I just witness?

Am I to tell anyone?

Do I believe my own eyes?

James and Simon came running noisily towards me. Simon had a beaker of wine and was spilling it as he is staggered.

"Hey there Jesus, are you sleeping? Now we are men we can drink wine – you should try it."

And with that, he tripped and threw the entire contents

over me. I stood dripping in what I could say smelt like strong vinegar. He scrambled to his feet, brushed himself down, looked at me then did the biggest belch ever. We three looked at each other and burst out laughing. we threw our arms around each other and sang a song while dancing in a circle of three.

The next morning, I awoke with my head in two places. I had enjoyed the wine and all the fun that went with it but I couldn't stop thinking about Nana. Was it the wine or am I truly blessed with an imaginary friend?

I fell out of my bed, washed my face and hands in a pail of cool water and decided to venture out into the morning sun.

"So then, what have you to say for yourself?" my father demanded.

"What for father?" I cautiously replied.

"Your disappearing act last night," he added.

I had to stop and think for a moment as my mind was all a bit of a blur.

"Well?" he shouted. "I'm waiting."

And with folded arms, he squared up to me. I knew I was in trouble. There was no way I was going to mention Nana as he would never believe me.

So I blurted. "It was all Simon's fault he demanded that I should try more wine now that I was a man."

A bit my top lip in hope.

"And you didn't think to let us know where you were? Was that Simon's fault too?"

He uncrossed his arms and walked towards me, now trying to cower backwards only to be stopped by a gatepost.

"We had no idea where you were. You could've been

dead in a ditch or hanging from a tree. We were sick with worry!!"

His face was redder than I have ever seen it and I felt ashamed.

"How were we to know you were in the synagogue, of all places, talking to the elders?"

He pulled back. He wasn't an angry type of man and this is the first time I'd seen him so upset.

"James and Simon wanted me to go back with them for more wine but on the way, we passed the synagogue and I heard the elders talking in large numbers and wanted to go and listen to them. So I left the boys and went in and sat listening and talking with the elders. I had no idea I was so long and I didn't want to wake you when I got home."

I bowed my head and apologised for being selfish. He grabbed me by the shoulders with both hands and looked me square in the face.

"YOU are special. YOU are our son. Your mother and I love you dearly and heaven knows what we would do if anything should happen to you."

He squeezed me so tight that I thought I would snap. As he loosened his grip he was shaking. His eyes desperately trying to hold back tears his bottom lip quivering.

"Now let there be no more said on the matter, we have work to do."

We smiled at each other and nodded in agreement. I decided from then on to stay away from wine; maybe have just a little at mealtimes or celebrations.

Our time together was taken up with crops and animals and my father teaching me more about carpentry. But I had discovered that I had a new skill and it occupied my mind for a good deal of my time.

I found I could be sleight of hand or appear to make things disappear then reappear. My mother was the easiest to fool, or so she made out! I couldn't help thinking that maybe I could control this new gift. My father said I shouldn't waste valuable time with such nonsense and get on with my chores.

I loved going to the synagogue and showing the elders some of my tricks. One time a bird with a poorly wing landed on the altar. I caught it, stroked it with my right hand and blessed it. After a few flaps of its wings, it flew with ease up to the rafters. Nothing was said but they all looked at each other in amazement. I was very pleased with myself. I smiled up at the roof and said *thank you*. I didn't know who I was saying it to but it felt right.

Another time, the elders couldn't light the candles as the flame kept dying out. I took a candle, held it up and closed my eyes. We felt a faint breeze blow and the candle was lit.

I must admit, these new skills did cause a stir amongst the elders, so I decided not to try any more tricks for a while.

It was at this point when I met a young man called John. He had seen me performing my little tricks and decided I was someone he wanted to be friends with.

We got on well together. We were roughly the same age and had the same views on the scriptures and the elders' stories. This made us want to take trips to the city of Jerusalem to try and further our knowledge. It was a long journey from Nazareth to Jerusalem and it wouldn't be until I was older that Mother and Father would give in and allow me to go wandering with John.

CHAPTER 5

18

I was 18 when John and I took our first trip to Jerusalem. My mother packed some bread, cheese and olives and my father gave us a big leather water holder. We packed it all onto one of Father's donkeys and set off into the vast unknown. It was strange to think that this donkey's father had carried my mother with me in her womb, on a similar journey.

As we were into our second day of travelling, we came across a one-legged beggar dressed in smelly, dirty rags lying by the side of the road. His lips were swollen and cracked, and swarms of flies were congregating around his eyes, nipping and irritating them.

As we got closer to him, he tried to sit up but weak with hunger and thirst, he couldn't. John went straight over to him with the water bottle and holding his head up, put the bottle to his lips. More water poured over him than he was able to swallow. I took some bread and wet it, pushing it gently to his mouth. He took a little and tried to chew it but choked. I tried again and this time he managed to take it. John gave him a little more water and between us, we managed to feed this poor wretch.

As we continued our journey, the further we went on, the more poor souls we encountered and as our supplies were limited, we could only help so many. The strange thing was, that just by acknowledging they were there and that we spoke to them, seemed to give them hope and a spark of humanity reignited in their lifeless eyes.

I have never noticed as many unfortunates as on this journey – my heart grew heavier with every meeting. John also found his heart crying for these people. We both felt helpless and this time, I had no tricks with which to help them. The closer to Jerusalem we got, the more there were.

As the city came into sight, we headed for the main gate. The gate was guarded by Romans. They were very hostile and decided between them who should go in and who shouldn't. It was a game they played to get over their boredom.

John, me and the donkey made our way forward and were immediately stopped by these bullies.

"What is your business here." One of the guards shouted.

John stepped up and told him we were going into the temple.

"Not today," the guard laughed, shoving John back

with his shield. John went to retaliate but I caught his shoulder.

"No, my brother, leave it; we can come back tomorrow!" I advised. I looked deep into the guard's eyes and he wiped them as if he had sand in them.

"Yes... yes. Come back tomorrow." The guard glanced back at me. I nodded and he nodded back.

We camped out that night and, in the morning, made out way back to the gate. The same guard was on duty. I nodded at him and he squinted, giving me a forced smile.

John and I went straight on through the gates. Compared to our town, the city was vast and so loud and vibrant with colour. It was breathtaking.

We walked in looking right and left our mouths open and our minds on fire trying to take it all in. The marketplace was huge; selling everything you could possibly imagine. I picked up a painted pot and the seller was on me like a viper. I quickly put it back and didn't touch anything else. We made our way through the crowds until we reached an inn. I tied the donkey to a post and John said he would go in and ask for a room whilst I waited outside.

A small child came over and looking at me with big brown eyes and cupped hands, asked for help. I reached into my bag and produced a piece of bread which the child snatched before scampering off into the crowds. Children are quick to learn and I was suddenly surrounded by a sea of little children, all begging for a morsel of food.

My heart sank as I knew I could do nothing to help them, so I asked them to sit down. I decided to tell them a story Nana had told me when I was their age. I could see that all they wanted was something to eat and drink. Our own supplies were low but I did have a few shekels in my bag. I told the children to stay there and I went into the inn, bought a loaf of bread and went back and sat down with them.

With a prayer in my heart, I started to tear off pieces of bread, giving each child a generous piece. I kept sharing and tearing but the loaf didn't seem to be getting any smaller. Still, I tore lumps off until all the little faces were happily munching away. I looked at the bread and still had half left. How could that be?

John reappeared from the inn, I stood up and the children ran away laughing and shouting.

"We have a room for seven nights," John told me, "which will be enough for us to celebrate Passover."

I thanked him and we led the donkey through the alley into a small stable where there was plenty of straw for him to munch on.

Exhausted after our journey, we went into the inn, sat at a table and ate a hearty stew of vegetables and bread, washed down with a flagon of mead. I've never tasted mead before and found it was nicer than wine. Fully satiated, we retired to our room, washed our hands and faces then flopped onto the straw cots. It was not long before I fell into a deep sleep.

When I awoke, I could hear a cockerel crowing in the distance. I looked over at John and he was still snoring away – loudly.

"He will be like that for a few minutes yet," said a voice that I knew so well.

"Nana!" I gasped and sure enough, there she was all radiant and glowing even more than last time. Now though, she was floating above the floor. I couldn't help but look under her feet to see if I could see the wall on the other side of the room. It was a very strange sensation.

"Fear not dear boy for I bring you great news."

I sat back folded my arms and crossed my legs to listen to what she was about to tell me.

"You are to be great friends with John. However, you will go your separate ways. He will be a great asset to your cause and you will love him like a brother."

"What cause is this Nana? Why John and why me? Yes, I do love him like a brother – we are united in our thoughts."

"One day your paths will cross again and that will be a great union for mankind. John will be the anointer and you the blessed." She paused and smiled a most radiant smile. "So, for now, I wish you well."

"Nana… Nana, what does all this mean?"

I found myself shouting at the ceiling and Nana had gone again.

John woke with a start and fell out of his cot.

"What…What? Who were you talking to?"

"No one," I said calmly. "I was dreaming and talking in my sleep. I'm sorry to wake you."

John clambered to his feet and gave an almighty stretch with a yawn to match. He rubbed his eyes and said, "I'm starving let's eat."

I was glad that he hadn't heard Nana or me talking.

All was well that day. It was Passover. A celebration that would last seven days. A very holy event, so having our breakfast early was lucky as for the rest of the celebration we could not eat any food made from grain, barley, oats or wheat with only sips of water.

We made our way through the streets to the synagogue, pushing and shoving through the crowds, with more pushing and shoving until we made it.

Once we reached the massive steps of the building, we climbed up, went through the huge wooden doors that opened up into the vast hall. It was swarming with people, like a beehive; the noise was immense. I'd never experienced anything quite like it as I was always told to be quiet in holy places.

Just as that thought escaped, there was a cry of "Silence… Silence."

The great hall immediately fell into a hush. The priest started his sermon and I was mesmerised. I could hear his deep, booming voice delivering word after word and I took it all in with relish. But as soon as it started it was

over and I was left feeling cheated; I wanted more. This was so much more intense than back home.

I suddenly felt like I belonged. I turned to John and he was staring into space, glassy-eyed, I tapped him on the shoulder.

"John…"

He continued to stare.

"John…"

He turned and looked at me with awe all over him.

"I am at one," he said under his breath.

Then burst out more loudly, "I am at one."

Then he grabbed both my hands and we spun around looking at each other laughing and laughing with sheer joy.

We made our way back to the inn, went straight

to our room and lay on our cots in silence.

The silence seemed to last forever before John said

"Were we really there?"

I pondered my answer.

"Yes."

It was a simple answer but it was enough.

We both continued staring at the ceiling until we drifted off to sleep.

The celebration carried on for seven days and each day was just as intense for us as the first. We joined in the Passover feast and spoke to many other people about the teachings we had heard.

On the seventh day, it was time to make our way home again. We gathered our belongings, retrieved and packed the donkey and started our walk home.

The journey seemed far less arduous; it felt easier, as if we had been made anew by the celebrations that week.

We had found something special, a deep bond and friendship that would go on to last a lifetime.

CHAPTER 6

20

I had noticed more and more my need to travel and spread the gospels of the Lord. John also had this calling and decided that he too should go out and spread the word. So, as Nana predicted, we parted company but remained together in our hearts and, although I would miss him, it just seemed the right thing to do.

I still helped my father with the animals and I was starting to get to grips with carpentry. Father was so patient, especially as my thoughts were elsewhere. Whenever I had spare time from helping Father and doing my daily chores, I sat with the elders, discussing the holy scriptures. The more we discussed, the deeper I wanted to delve. I had always had questions beyond my years but my search for more knowledge and understanding was never quenched by the answers I was given. My thirst for knowledge grew like a vine and stretched far beyond that held by the elders in my temple.

Sometimes I would take myself off to one of the surrounding villages to try other temples and sermons. Every now and then, I would try to learn about other religious beliefs. It seemed to me that we all have our God but we see him with different eyes. I found myself in trouble once by joining in a debate with some Roman soldiers who were camped nearby. Romans were a very strong people who worshipped many gods – they had gods for various things such as a god for war, another for the sea, even one for wine. This reminded me of when we lived in Egypt as the Egyptians also had many gods. It was not a new concept to me, yet I found it strange.

I tried to tell the Romans about my God and help them receive him into their lives. Their drunk and violent ways overtook their hearts, and when they became aggressive about receiving my words, I knew that I should leave.

There was one in the group though who was not so hostile. He had a gentler nature and when his companions stood to move me on, he calmed them and put his hand on my shoulder.

"Leave them. They are war-weary and have nothing but anguish and pain in their hearts. You are a good man, and I listened to your words but, here, you are trying to break a rock with a twig."

As our eyes met, a calm filled us both, as though we were family. I thanked him and started my way back home. It was getting late and soon the people of the night would be taking to the streets. I had tried talking to these people too, to teach them about my God, but my sermons could not reach them. It felt as if I needed to strengthen my own belief in my sermons before trying to ask others to believe them and welcome a change. I now felt like my mission was beginning. A mission to help others see what I saw.

One night, while having a meal with my mother and father, I started talking about my future and both said in unison, "You are a special young man."

They looked at each other and we laughed for a few moments realising that our family bond was strong. My father then gathered himself, took my hand and looked deep into my eyes.

"When you were born, we were told that you would be a special person. We had no reason to deny it but have always wondered why? Why us? Why you? And as you have grown, you have shown an ability to calm a situation or show incredible compassion.

At first, we thought this could not be right but now, as the years have gone by, we have grown to accept it more and more."

His eyes searched my face with a look of love and joy in them. My mother joined him in holding my hands then she spoke.

"My son. My darling boy. Every mother sees their son as a foundation to help keep the family together. To be strong. We see this in you. You have made us better people and the knowledge you have gained in your travels and searches has been passed onto us. You have an amazing ability with words and wisdom to help soften the soul and ease the mind. I do not want to lose you or never see your beautiful face but, if you feel the need to go out and spread the word. then so be it. Go and spread the word of the Lord."

CHAPTER 7

28

I had no idea that my father had passed away as I was still on my venture so there was no way to get the sad news to me. I had been so wrapped up in my mission that going home was never considered but I was always there in my mind.

And then I did go home. My mother broke the news to me and I didn't take it very well. I had helped countless poor unfortunate souls in their lives, yet, when it came to mine, I could do nothing. So, I did what I do best; I prayed.

I asked God to receive him and care for him.

I asked God to help me understand this.

I asked God to care for my mother when I left again.

I asked God to…

I had no more words.

For the second time in my life, I had lost someone dear

to me. This was now making my understanding of loss even stronger. By suffering myself, I could understand the suffering of others.

Once again, my mother had to bid me farewell as my mission called me. My understanding of God's help was needed more and more in the world and, if I was to succeed in this quest, I would gratefully accept all of his help.

I travelled throughout the land, walking many miles and crossing many plains, preaching and giving sermons. I was beginning to gather followers and people started calling me 'Rabbi'. More and more, I seemed to have the ability to heal, strengthen or supply the needy.

One day I arrived at a small village to speak to the people. A blind man was sitting in the crowd and, as everyone listened to my sermon, he became agitated. He got up to leave and his movements disturbed them. They jeered and scolded him for banging into them.

I called to him, "You there, blind man. Please wait."

He stopped, facing away from me. I went through the crowd to him and touched his shoulder.

"Why do you leave with such haste and anger?"

He turned to face me and said, "I am sorry Rabbi but I cannot listen to you anymore. You speak of wondrous things that I can never see and it is hurting my heart because my faith can never be as strong as yours."

A wave of emotion came over me and I felt an overwhelming desire to help this man see the wonderful world in which we lived.

I took both of his hands and said "Do you welcome God?"

He hesitated for a minute and then nodding, he said, "with all my heart."

I put my hands over his eyes and said, "then you already see God. You just needed to proclaim it."

I removed my hands and kissed his eyes.

He began to shake and cry. He put his hands to his eyes and looked at them. He fell to his knees and said, "I do see… I can see the way! All these years I have been blind and now I see the way. Thank you, Rabbi. Thank you."

He grabbed my feet sobbing until his eyes were tear-drenched. All around, the people stood and looked on in amazement. I took his arms and helped him to his feet and he shook my hand, smiling. He turned and raised his hands to the crowd, who cheered and clapped, singing the praises of the Lord.

I turned and slipped away.

"Excuse me, young man."

It was a voice that I would recognise anywhere. I turned and there was Nana, beautiful as ever. She seemed to be younger every time she visited.

"What a wonderful thing to do for that man," she said in her soft, angelic voice. I smiled and stared for what felt like ages, then gathered myself.

"Nana, can I help these people? Do I really have the power to heal, to provide, to help my fellow man?"

I was feeling in need of reassurance as it was hard coming to terms with my abilities.

"As I told you before, you are special. You are chosen to go forward and spread the word. Open the hearts and minds of the people. Let them see what you see. Help them live better lives with God."

"Oh Nana, it seems such a huge task. To show my fellow man the light and the way to God."

I felt exhausted by my words and bowed my head.

"The journey will be met with many obstacles but have no fear, my son, you will overcome them. You will help all who need help. You will light the way."

She blew me a kiss and, as usual, faded away into the light.

I was energised. I was ready. I would go out and meet the World. I was going to spread the word of the Lord.

***

I had heard that my friend John was now living in the Jordan Valley. He had kept the promise that we had made to each other to spread the word of the Lord by baptising his followers in the River Jordan. I decided that my next journey would be to Jordan.

It took me four days to walk to the river and then another two days to find John. As I approached him, he recognised me straight away and without hesitation, he came running towards me, arms outstretched with tears in his eyes. He crashed into me with such force that we both fell to the ground.

"Jesus. Jesus, is it really you?"

"Yes… Yes, it is."

The sound of his words was muffled due to us still being in a pile on the ground. Then he smiled and we both scrambled up, brushed ourselves down and stood staring at each other.

It had been a few years since we had made the pledge and then parted. We were now both long-haired, bearded men.

"Come Jesus."

He took my arm led me along the river to a clearing where he had made a small tent and living area. He pulled back the canvas and showed me in. It was just big enough for us both to stand up in. There was a bed of straw and some animal skins on the floor.

"Please sit. My home is your home."

He reached over to a jug and beaker filled it with clean, fresh water, handing it to me, saying, "I hear you have been doing wonderful work, making my job more needed. People have been coming here every day to be baptised. I have done as we vowed to spread the word."

The look in his eyes was of pure sincerity and joy. You could tell that this man was at one with God and at peace with himself.

I finished my water and gave him the beaker back, saying, "You filled my cup. I drank from it. It was needed; now my thirst is no more. This is what we need to tell the people. You and I. By spreading God's word through the holy scriptures, we can help those who seek the way."

"Jesus, please. I am not worthy to be compared to you. I am but a humble man who has taken the vow to spread the word. I am your servant here at your command."

He bowed his head low.

"Thank you, John, please get up. I am no more than you. We are both God's messengers with a long task ahead of us."

We both stood up, put our arms on each other's shoulders and smiled. We went outside. It was getting dark and the stars were filling the sky.

"Look up John. Look up to the heavens. The sky is wide and black, yet the stars can be seen shining through. If we can make that happen down here on Earth, then all we have set out to do will not be in vain."

John stared up and clasped his hands. He closed his eyes and started to weep.

"So vast. So many stars. We do have a task, don't we!"

"All we have to do is keep the faith John and that will get us through."

We stood staring for a while until our eyes could stay open no longer then went back into the tent and slept peacefully till morning.

We were woken by loud voices singing and laughing, so looking at each other bewildered, we went outside to see what the commotion was. As we came out of the tent, the crowd hushed and all eyes were on us. Then an elder came forward, leaning heavily on his staff.

"This is our family. We have travelled many miles to seek the one they call John. Please, is one of you him?" he asked.

A group of people stood around the elder. Some young, some old, women carrying children, children running in and out. All with looks of hope through expectant eyes.

John stood forward, arms outstretched in welcome, "It is me you're looking for. I am John."

The crowd moved forward to him and the elder bowed his head and cried a sigh of relief. John went to him to comfort him.

"Have you all come to receive the way?"

The elder looked up at John through large brown eyes and nodded.

The crowd cheered and laughed. I stood back as John went to the family one by one, shaking hands and making them all welcome. John told the elder that the family should rest for a while to prepare themselves for what would take place.

"I am glad that you are here Jesus. Now you can witness true wonder. The ceremony of baptism."

John went over to the elder and asked if his people were ready.

"Yes, we are ready and we are all very grateful for what you are about to do. Bless you, my son."

John looked around at the family's faces, each with an excited smile, waiting for his command. Once again John held up his hands.

"Welcome… Welcome, everyone. Today will be the beginning of your new lives. I can give you hope. I can give you guidance. But you must have it in your heart to believe. It is up to you to follow the way of the Lord."

John turned and walked into the water up to his waist, then he turned around and said, "Come. Come into the water. Don't be afraid, I will help you."

The crowds, eager but hesitant, moved slowly down to

the riverbank and the first young man went splashing in.

John turned him around to face the others and shouted.

"In the name of the Father, I baptise thee!"

And without a pause for breath, he pulled the young man back into the water and straight up again. The young man gave a gasp and a splutter, threw his arms up and cried, "Praise the Lord for I am reborn."

One by one, the rest of the family went splashing into the river, even the children helped by the others. John baptised them all apart from the elder who remained on the shore.

"What troubles you Father? Come on in," shouted his son.

"I fear I cannot as I am too unsteady."

He looked ashamed as he watched his family but couldn't risk going in.

"Do not worry. Stay there." John smiled, "I'll come to you."

He waded out and went up to the elder.

"Do not worry. I can perform the task on land."

And with that, he dipped his hand in the water and touched the elder's forehead and whispered, "In the name of the Lord almighty, I baptise thee."

The elder's face lit up and he reached for the heavens and shouted, "Thank you. Thank you."

All his family gathered around him and they hugged each other.

John left them to celebrate and came over to me.

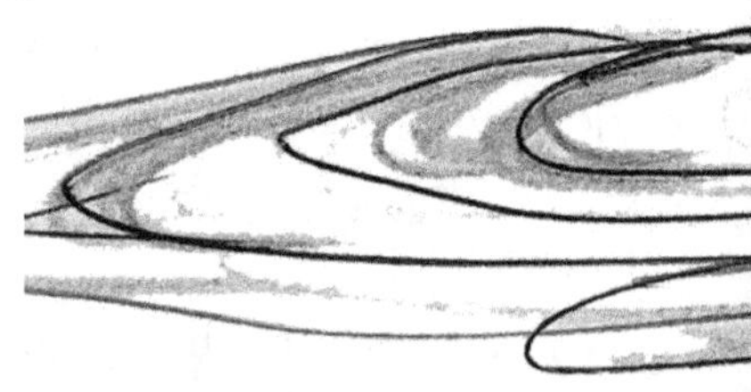

"Isn't it a wonderful sight?" He was completely fulfilled by his actions and I felt that I too should take this vow.

"Please John, can I go into the water to be baptised by you?"

He looked at me in astonishment. Eyes wide and his mouth open.

"But you are the Lamb of God. How can I do this for you?"

"Please John. What I witnessed here today was truly amazing and I want to be a part of it, to make me whole."

I could see by John's face that he was struggling with the thought of this task and he paced left and right, tugging on his beard and mumbling. Then he stopped and looked me square in my face and kissed my cheek.

"Your will is my will. I am your servant. I will be honoured to do this for you."

We both walked towards the water and John led the way into the water up to his waist and I followed. He grabbed my shoulders and turned me around to face the bank.

Then shouted at the top of his voice, "In the name of the Father, I baptise thee."

And his words echoed loud all around and the family came to witness. When I surfaced, my heart and my lungs were bursting and I could hear cheering and clapping. I had been baptised by John.

John the Baptist.

It was as though heaven had opened up and hordes of angels were singing.

We started to make our way out of the water and clambered back up the riverbank. I fell to my knees held my arms out. Closed my eyes and paid homage to the Lord.

My Lord God Almighty.

John had made me true and I felt a whole new fire spreading through my veins. My head swam with this newfound blessing. I needed to get away and take stock of myself, for the way of the Lord God was now even stronger in me.

Once again, John and I parted. I left him by the river doing what John did best. I was glad that I had found him again – it was good to see an old friend – but I needed to move on.

I filled my water bag and headed off. If I was to try and cleanse my head and my body, it seemed natural to do it in a desolate place. The desert.

CHAPTER 8

30

I walked on and on until I found a small clearing at the top of a high ridge and this made me feel a little closer to heaven. I looked down at the vast desert. It was an unforgiving, unloved place and this is where I would stay for as long as it would take me to feel ready.

I only had one water bag and one loaf of bread. I had to ration myself to small pieces and sips of water so that I could last longer.

The first few days seemed to come and go without a problem. My rations were holding out and my willpower was still strong. But it was the heat of the day that became sometimes unbearable. I had little shade, just a big rock which, as the sun passed it, gave me some shelter.

I spent most of my time in prayer which comforted me through the day. At night, it strangely would become very cold and even the rock could not hold the heat of the sun. As I had no means to make a fire, I curled up like a baby to try to keep warm. Sometimes, on a really hot day, I thought I could see people walking or hear laughing but it was just my mind starting to wander and play tricks on me.

That is until one night when there was a big, full moon giving light all around and a shadow appeared in front of my rock. I stared at the shadow for a few moments and it started to move, then a voice spoke.

"How long do you think you can carry on like this?"

Startled, I stood up.

"Who's there? Show yourself."

The shadow stayed motionless.

"Do not fear as I come in peace and offer you help."

My eyes searched the area but I still saw no one. This time I knew it was not Nana.

"Why do you hide? Will you not face me so that I can see you?"

I was intrigued as to who this helper was.

"Why do you suffer so? You have the power; why don't you use it? Why not turn one of those boulders into a nice loaf of bread?"

The voice was very soft. Tempting. I suddenly realised I was being tested by evil.

"Do not try to tempt me. I have come to make peace with myself. Yes, I have the power but I cannot use it in a moment

of weakness for personal gain. So go – leave me be."

I still couldn't see anyone. The voice spoke again.

"Very well. But you could do it, couldn't you?"

A cloud passed over the moon and it became dark and the voice became silent. I felt a shiver run down my spine.

I fell to my knees and looked to the heavens.

I pleaded, "Oh merciful father. Am I to be tempted as well as endure this test? If this is how it must be, then I shall try to be strong."

Then the cloud passed the moon allowing its light to shine through the darkness again.

I had started to lose track of the days I had spent here. So, I started scratching on the rock with a piece of flint, marking each day as it passed. My test of faith was making me feel strong but the desire to eat and drink was becoming stronger. The water bag was emptying rapidly and the bread was long gone. At night rock insects came out. They were easy to catch. I was unsure at first but as my hunger took hold and I thought of what the voice had said, I had no choice but to eat them.

One day, as the sun reached its peak in the middle of the day and the rock gave little protection, the voice reappeared.

"Although the rock is big and solid, it offers you little shelter. Why not come with me? I will give you shelter so that your body does not suffer."

The sun was bearing down upon me and had it not been for the rock giving some shade, I would have been badly burnt. The shadow came over the rock giving more refuge from the searing sun.

"See. Here is my help. Come join me and I will give you all the kingdoms that you desire. Just go into the shade and we shall rule together."

I stared at the shade and it looked inviting but I could never leave my Lord God for another.

"This is evil; why do you tempt me like this? I have come here to find myself and become closer to God. All you want to do is to trick me away from him."

Sweat ran into my eyes as the sun beat down. My throat was dry and the shadow looked tempting but I was determined to stay true.

"No, you are evil and I will never join you. Your temptation shows you for who you are and that you rule with shame and deceitful ways. I want to live a good and honest life."

"So be it. Think of my offer to you. If you change your mind, I will be waiting."

The long dark shadow disappeared and the protective shade was reduced to that which the rock provided. Slowly I moved towards it and sat with my back to the rock. I closed my eyes.

"Oh Father, am I doing the right thing? Am I going in the right direction? This evil playing with me is testing me so hard that my thoughts are becoming jumbled. Please give me a little guidance please so that I can continue alone with my quest."

I was exhausted, tired, hungry and thirsty. I had scratched many marks on the rock. I made myself stand up and move so that my limbs did not seize. I shuffled up and down my makeshift home, trying to clear my head with prayer. Then, a beam of light hit the rock and a sweet scent filled the air. I turned and there she was in all her radiance. Nana.

I was desperate to hug her as she was the most welcome sight I have ever seen but I knew she was not there in body but as a spirit. I stared at her, even though my eyes were glassy and my vision blurred. My swollen, cracked lips gave her as much of a smile as they could muster.

"I have come to give you hope Jesus, for you have nearly reached the end of your trial. Your suffering will make you strong. It will help you understand the plight of others so that you can offer them the way and help them to be strong and call upon the Lord God for guidance. Be brave Jesus. For your courage will be needed when the time comes. God is with you."

She smiled her beautiful smile and left.

I just stood and stared at the area where she appeared and my mind was at peace. I lay down on the ground behind the rock and slept.

More days passed and the scratches were growing in number. I counted them and found I had been there for thirty-five days. I knew I could not bear much more. I started to think about leaving – I had endured enough to help my cause.

But that night, just as I was falling asleep, a bitter cold

came over me and I knew that he was here again.

"What do you want now? Haven't I suffered enough? Yet you feel the need to try to tempt me again?"

I looked around but there was no one there even though the evil chill pervaded. I sat and waited, drawing my skinny legs up to my chest.

Then the voice spoke, "Yes, you have suffered. Yes, you have endured. And yes, it has made you a wiser man. But did you have to do this to prove yourself? What is your God if he expects you to do this for him?"

His words ran through my head and I felt hurt at every word he said.

"My God didn't tell me to do this or expect it of me. I took it upon myself to show my devotion to him."

My sore cracked lips bled as I spoke.

"See how he makes you suffer. Why doesn't he heal your lips? If you come with me, you will never know pain or suffering again."

He was right; I had endured pain, suffering and all in my heavenly father's name. But this was a test. A test of my faith I took upon myself to show that I have faith.

Yes, I have faith.

"Once again, you try me with your empty words. Test me no more, as I now realise my faith is strong and that, wherever I go, my God goes with me. I won't listen to you anymore. Your words are nothing to me. I shall only hear the words of the Lord God."

"Very well, I will leave you. But mark my words Jesus of Nazareth, I will be there in every shadow, watching and waiting. Every chance I have, I will choose someone new to join me. They will be weak and come to me willingly, for humans are weak and my ways are strong. We will meet again."

What had just happened?

Had I just fought with the forces of evil?

I did not know. But I did feel that my strength to resist had weakened him.

The following day I went to scratch on the rock and as I counted the scratches, I saw they added up to 40. My work here was done. I had the spirit within me and my evil was gone.

It was time to go back down the mountain, to leave the desert and join my fellow man.

The journey back to civilisation was hard. I was physically weak but mentally and spiritually I was stronger than I had ever been.

I kept going until I found a clear stream with trees and soft earth. The colours were almost too much for my sunburnt eyes. I took in everything that was around me. The beauty of the trees. The smell of the flowers and patches of soft grass. My senses had been heightened and I felt safe in the fact that I was here and away from the desert.

I looked around for signs of life but there were none. No broken twigs. No footprints. No noise.

I made my way down to the water's edge and slowly and painfully removed my clothing. I looked down at my now frail frame.

I walked towards the cool water and waded in up to my

waist. I am not a swimmer; I just wanted to cleanse myself of my turmoil and the desert dust. It felt wonderful and I splashed around for a while. It was a freshwater stream, so I drank my fill. I got out and sat on a rock to dry off. There were small fish in the stream. I caught some and ate them raw. I didn't like killing them but it was survival and it seemed like they were there for me. It was nice to have something other than rock bugs and they tasted good.

I dressed and followed the stream for a while until I came to a man-made clearing. There was smoke climbing up through the trees. I made my way over to find a small settlement with a few huts and animals. Walking towards its centre, I could hear someone giving a sermon. I headed in that direction and found a group of people sitting in a circle listening to a preacher. I stood at the back by a fence and listened to what he had to say and was delighted to hear him preach the Word of our Lord God. He seemed very knowledgeable and held the crowd in his hand. When he had finished and the crowd dispersed, I went to him and asked his name.

"I am Simon. Who are you friend, although I feel that I know you already?"

"My name is Jesus. Jesus of Nazareth."

He fell to the floor and held my feet.

"Please Simon, get up," I pleaded.

"But MasterI am not worthy to stand in your presence."

He bowed his head rubbing his hands together.

"Simon, you seem to know the way very well. Your sermon was most enjoyable. I am travelling to the sea of Galilee; would you like to come with me?"

"My Lord I would love to come. But I am to help here

in the village. As soon as I am done, I can come and join you there."

There was a look of hope in his eyes. He seemed an honest man, so I agreed.

"That is a perfect idea Simon. Finish your business here and join me when you can."

We shook hands and he asked me to his home for a meal. His hospitality was welcome and I left nourished, starting back on my journey with renewed vigour.

Some fishermen were working their nets and getting ready for their daily sail. I decided to go speak with them.

"Morning," I said with no expectation.

"Morning to you," they replied.

"Are you looking for work?" one asked.

"Thank you but no. I was just interested," I said seriously.

They carried on.

"Is being a fisherman a hard job?"

I was trying to show my interest but couldn't find the words.

Laughing, he said, "It's a thankless task. We make our nets, fix our boat, go out and get very wet and cold. Sometimes we catch nothing or very little yet we know there are fish we have seen them."

"I would like to go out with you. Just to see what it's like as I've never been on the water."

I was suddenly excited.

"Well, if you don't get in the way and don't fall in I

suppose it can't do any harm. This is Andrew and I am Peter."

He extended his powerful arm with a solid handshake.

"My name is Jesus," I said as I was being shaken by the fisherman's strong grip.

"I've heard of you? Are you the travelling Rabbi from Nazareth?"

I was taken aback by his comment. To think that news can travel that far so quickly.

"Yes. That's me."

"Well, Jesus of Nazareth, let's take you for your first boat experience. Just be careful not to fall in," Peter laughed.

Then he threw the net into the boat and pushed it into the sea, jumping in when he could. It was a cool, breezy day; the wind was gentle but strong enough to take us out. It was very exciting. After a while, he stood up and grabbed the net.

"This is where you earn your ride," he chuckled.

Andrew and I helped throw the huge net over the side and we sat back and waited.

And waited.

And waited.

"What exactly are we waiting for?" I asked.

"Well, as we drift along, the fish get caught in the net and hopefully, the boat will start to lean over with the weight of a large catch," said Andrew.

But still, we waited.

"We must have a good catch today as we need to feed our families. Our supplies are running low," shouted Peter to the net. "Come on fish, help a poor fisherman survive."

"Have you ever tried a prayer?"

"If I thought it would help, I would shout it from the mast top," he jested, throwing up his arms to the sky.

"Well try now," I suggested.

"I suppose it couldn't do any harm could it?" he shrugged.

He got down on his knees and clasped his hands saying loudly in a sarcastic voice. "Oh Lord, if you can hear me, please fill my net with fish. How was that?"

"Do you believe in what you have asked for Peter?"

He nodded with a squint of uncertainty.

"Of course I do. I have always been a believer in the Lord."

And with that, the boat gave a sharp turn to the right and nearly threw us all overboard. Startled, we made a quick grab at the net and started trying to heave it in but it was too heavy. The expression on Peter's face was one of shock.

"We will have to sail back to the closest shore and drag the net along until we can beach it. Quick brothers grab the oars." There was a sound of urgency in his voice.

Andrew and I grabbed the oars and started to row back to shore. We pulled and pulled while Peter steered and sorted the sail until we slowly made our way back to the shore. We hit land with a scraping thud. The net was glittering and bulging with splashing fish of all shapes and sizes. Andrew leapt out and tied a rope around a tree to secure the boat. The other two of us jumped out into the water to try and gather the catch but it seemed we were fighting a losing battle.

It was at this moment three other fishermen were

walking by and saw that we were having trouble. They ran over to help and we all hauled in the net with its contents spilling out onto the land. After securing the net and its contents, we all sat back, mopped our brows and took long swigs from the water bags. We stared at each other in awe.

Peter spoke first.

"I have been a fisherman as long as I can remember and never had a catch so great."

We all smiled and nodded looking at each other with satisfaction. He stood and went to the three men and offered his hand in thanks.

"And I must thank you brothers for arriving just in time."

"You are welcome, brother. We were only too glad to help with such an amazing catch. You must be truly blessed," said the first.

The second also accepted Peter's hand and agreed. Then there was silence and all eyes were on me.

"So, the rumours are true? You really can work miracles?" Peter said as he sat back down. "It was you wasn't it?"

"Did you not ask the Lord for help?" I replied.

He nodded.

"And you say you are a believer?"

He nodded again.

"So, who was it who helped you? Not me!"

As I looked into his face, I could see his mind working, as were the others rubbing their beards trying to understand.

"If you are a believer and call on the Lord, he will help.

I just helped you to see that."

Their faces shone in amazement. The first stranger stood up.

"My name is James. I am a fisherman."

The second also stood up, "My name is John. I too am a fisherman."

The third, seeming more excited said proudly, "I am Philip. We have heard of you Rabbi and believe that you are the Lamb of God and we wish to join you."

I was touched by these words. I needed some company. So the six of us stood up and in a circle, we linked arms and danced around on the wet sand, smiling with glee at our new-found friendship.

Then falling onto the sand in exhaustion I said, "I am travelling through the land. Would you like to come with me?"

They all looked at each other with big excited eyes, smiling and nodding to each other.

"Then you shall all be fishers of men together."

Now I had five travelling companions: Peter; Andrew; John; James and Philip.

Together we started out on a new adventure.

<hr>

After getting supplies and a donkey, the men had to say goodbye to their wives and children with promises of their return. Leaving their families was not easy for them but they each accepted it as part of their destiny to make this journey. I knew I was asking a lot of these families.

We headed out to the far-off point at the southern

side of Galilee. It would take a few days to get there as the terrain was very hilly and there was no straight road to follow. We were in good spirits and, apart from our supplies, travelled light. We had our meals and slept out under the heavens.

As we continued our journey, we had stopped and made camp as the sun turned into a big orange ball as it slowly set behind the hills. It was here that we came across a group of men who seemed lost.

"Brothers," I beckoned in a friendly way so as not to cause alarm. "Brothers, are you lost?"

They stopped and looked at us.

"Please brother, we have travelled on this rugged path to find the man they call Jesus. Do you know of him?"

I moved forward and stretched out my hand and straightaway they knew who I was. They bowed down low, which made me very uncomfortable.

"Stand please; there is no need for you to bow. Tell me your names. I am Jesus of Nazareth, the one you are looking for."

"We are three normal men who wish to be shown the way. Will you help us, Lord?"

They rose to their feet, astonished.

"My name is Bartholomew. This is James and he is Thaddeus," said the first man.

I nodded to them and shook hands with each of them.

"We have heard all about your travels, your miracles and sermons; this is why we want to join you." James, who was the youngest, explained.

I turned to face my three companions.

"Shall we let them join us?" I asked.

They all agreed, so I held out both my arms, saying, "Welcome my friends. Welcome. Come sit by the fire and help yourself to water, bread and fish."

I didn't have to say it twice; they were hungry and thirsty from their journey and dived straight in. We spent a pleasant night by the fire talking and then slept peacefully. In the morning, we packed up, put out the fire, said our prayers and started off again.

We travelled for many days until we came upon the city of Jerusalem where we could restock our supplies and visit the temple there. The Romans held the city and there were soldiers everywhere. We were quite a large group that could draw attention – not a wise thing to happen. We tried to remain undetected but, unfortunately, this didn't happen and, sure enough, two guards came over to us.

"You! What is your business here?" asked one.

His manner was hostile and our group huddled together.

"We are on a pilgrimage around Galilee. We are peaceful and don't want to cause any trouble." I said convincingly.

"What's your name, Jew?"

There was suspicion in his voice.

"I am Jesus of Nazareth," I replied.

"So, it is true, you do exist. We have heard a lot about you, Jew."

His words were threatening and bitter. The Romans do not know our God and have started to believe that we are a threat.

"Well, don't let me hear from you and you won't get into any trouble."

He shoved my left shoulder. I touched my forehead and my chest and offered him my hand in friendship. He just pushed it away, spat on the ground, turned on his heels and walked off with his companion laughing and making comments about us.

I turned to the group. "Well, this is what we are up against. Do not let them get to you. Be strong. Keep the faith. Stay out of trouble and we will be fine. Now let's go to the temple first before we get our supplies. I think we should leave soon as possible; it will be dark soon and I don't think this is the place I want to stay for too long."

We made our way to the temple, tied the donkey up outside and entered. There were a lot of people coming and going and it was so noisy. It reminded me of the first time I visited this temple but this was different. There were Roman guards around the entrance. They were watching over the tables of moneylenders. There were many different tradesmen selling everything from rope to small animals. There were people making deals, selling crops and wine.

I couldn't believe what I was seeing; it was shocking. This has become a trade house – a den of thieves and robbers. My companions and I stared in disbelief. I could hold back no longer. I lunged forwards and tipped over the nearest table, then another and another. I was angry at what they had done to God's house.

I stood on a table and began to shout, "this is God's house. You turn it into a den of thieves and robbers! Get out and take your spoils with you. Never enter this house again!"

I was almost crazed and spitting my words out, finding it difficult to emphasise my feelings strongly enough. People were running and shouting. Birds, goats and chickens were running amok. Opportunists were scrambling for the coinage on the animal soiled floor. The guards couldn't believe what was going on and started to round everybody up.

My companions realised what was happening, grabbed me and quickly moved me to a side door. We crept down the side alley, hoping not to be seen.

Peter whispered, "what was that all about? I know they shouldn't be trading in there but did you have to make such a scene?"

I looked at Peter puzzled and said "Do you not understand Peter?"

He searched my face and I realised that he didn't.

"This is a house of prayer Peter and I will not have them desecrating it."

He hung his head and apologised.

We waited in the alley for a while until the commotion died down and made our way back to the front of the temple. Luckily our donkey was still where we had left him.

Suddenly the big wooden doors opened and out walked a clean-cut young man. We stood looking at each other for a moment and then I made the first move.

"Hello friend, are you of this house." I enquired.

He looked at me without smiling or any sign of passion.

"I am of no house; I am my own man."

"Then why are you here in God's house?"

The man stood very straight and like an unmovable pillar.

"I have come to meet you. The one they call Jesus. I have heard lots of stories about you. So I wanted to see you, see what you were like, but you just look, well, normal."

His face changed into one of confusion.

"What did you expect? A halo and wings?" I joked.

With this, he cracked a smile, albeit a pained one.

"So, why are you here?" he asked.

"We are on a journey around Galilee. We needed supplies and wished to visit the temple. What is your name?"

He drew a breath and said, "My name is Matthew and I am a tax collector before you ask."

"Well, that would explain your cold approach. That must be a thankless task."

He looked at everyone through narrowed eyes and shrugged, saying, "Someone has to do it."

"It's been nice talking to you Matthew but we must be on our way. We have a long journey ahead and now I have upset the locals and moneylenders we should leave."

He stepped aside and we filed past, trying not to look him in the eye. Tax collectors were not very well-liked. Matthew came and stood in front of us.

"I'm not a bad man you know. I'm just doing a job."

A murmur went around the group and someone chuckled.

"I can make a fire and bake bread too," he added, almost forlornly.

"What is it that you would like to say Matthew? Why are you here?"

"Take me with you," he blurted.

"Please take me with you. I won't be any trouble. I just want to learn the way."

Everybody stopped and looked at me.

I turned to Matthew and said, "Do you believe in God?"

He shrugged and shuffled his feet like a lost little boy.

"Do you *want* to believe in God?" I added.

Staring at me with piercing eyes, "Yes. Yes, I do. I want to belong. I want to be part of your world. I want to…"

He stopped and softened.

"I want to feel the way that I should feel – part of something special. I understand if you don't want me to come along though."

His stature changed from upright to humble.

"My friend, all you had to do was say the words and the Lord God would be with you. Of course you can join us – the more the merrier."

Although saying that, I wasn't actually expecting much merriment from him. A big beaming smile took over his face. He was like an excited puppy, not knowing where to stand or who to go to first. The whole group welcomed him and he calmed down.

As we moved out, supplies bought, we had to pass the guards at the main gate. So, we made ourselves ready for any abuse or confrontation we might face. Heads down, we started to file out when, sure enough, the same Roman guard we encountered when we arrived came forward.

"Hey, Jew. What have you stolen? Let me look in those bags."

He took out his dagger and was just about to rip open a sack of grain when Matthew stepped up.

"Malchus. Malchus, my friend. How is your mother these days?"

The Roman was surprised and stepped back.

"Matthew? What are you doing here with this rabble?"

Matthew grabbed the Roman's forearm.

"Malchus, these are my new friends and we are leaving the city. Please give my regards to your mother."

The guard stepped aside, re-sheathed his knife and waved us on. He was speechless as he turned and went back to his station, looking slightly confused.

After about twenty minutes, we stopped and circled Matthew. He looked concerned but kept his cool. His eyes looked left and right waiting for something to happen.

"Matthew, how on Earth did you manage that? You were as cool as mountain water yet slick as olive oil!"

Then everybody patted him on his shoulders, nearly knocking him over. There were chants of *Well done! Our hero*. It seemed that Matthew had found companionship.

As we journeyed, we taught him the Scriptures, told him stories and he received it all with a new light in his heart. As time went on, he softened and his tough exterior was no longer needed.

CHAPTER 9

31

One night, we were camped out as usual, with a big fire for warmth and the starry heavens for a roof. We sat in a bonded circle going over the day's events.

The next day we travelled to a town called Cana. It was an uneventful journey crossing the desert plains. Hot in the day, cold at night and no protection from either. Seeing the small town for the first time was a very welcome sight.

We set up camp on the outskirts of Cana and once settled, we went into town to gather supplies. There were Roman guards keeping an eye on the comings and goings.

Each of us knew our role and went our separate ways in smaller groups to attract less attention. As usual, Peter and Matthew accompanied me and the three of us slowly made our way around the bustling, dusty market stalls. I was not very good at haggling with the tradesmen, so I left that to Matthew. He could sell sand.

As we wandered around, we noticed a young man

following us. He tried in vain to disguise the fact that he was. Peter and Matthew wanted to surprise him in an alley to find out his intentions. I suggested we did it in the open where there would be witnesses in case his intentions were bad. It was decided that we would split up and go to three separate tradesmen within sight of each other to see what he did. After a few minutes of looking at a Persian rug which the tradesman was trying desperately to sell me, the young man approached me. I was on my guard and as he drew nearer, I suddenly turned to face him. Peter and Matthew came up behind him and blocked his escape. I decided to play it calm.

"Good morning. Can I help you?"

He stood there staring in disbelief at being discovered.

"Your tracking skills are not your best quality. I assume that there is a motive to your following us?"

He looked over his shoulder at Peter and Matthew and spluttered, "I'm sorry. I meant no harm. I was hoping you were someone I'd heard of. So I came to see for myself."

I looked at him. He was reasonably clean, hair well-kempt and he didn't look like much a rogue to me.

"Who do you think I am?" I asked.

"You're the healer; Rabbi Jesus? It's all over town that you're here and everyone knows what you do."

I looked around the market and faces looked away as I met their gaze. I hadn't noticed the side glances or heard their whispers but now that the lad had brought it to our attention, it was obvious.

"Are you Jesus the Rabbi?"

I looked at Peter and Matthew and they looked around

the faces of the other people too. It was now obvious that I was recognised, so there was no need to deny it.

"Yes, I am Jesus. Jesus of Nazareth. But I am not a Rabbi, just a deliverer of sermons to help people find the way."

The young man clasped his hands in excitement and went down on his knees.

"Then bless you, Jesus. If all the stories that I have been told of you are true, then you really are a special man!"

And with that, he stood up, looked at Peter and Matthew, smiled and ran off into the now gathering crowd. They turned to face them. Trying to block their advances.

Now some were chanting, "The Messiah. The Messiah is here. God be praised."

This caught the attention of the Roman guards and they started to intervene, trying to disperse the crowd. But the people were having none of it. I tried to calm them by raising my hands and standing on a trader's box, so I was raised above them. The crowd quietened and all faces were on me. I looked at them with a smile and my hands held out. They stared in expectancy, waiting for me to say something. When I started to speak, I had no idea what I was going to say but my words just came out. Words of comfort and joy, and praise to our God.

I ended with, "Now go. Go and spread the word of our Lord. Go in peace."

They slowly turned and went about their business. But there seemed to be a new calm and happiness about them.

"Well, that went well," Peter exclaimed.

"I thought that we were done for when those guards arrived," added Matthew.

Just then, a friendly-looking man approached.

"Excuse me Rabbi but I was wondering if you would like to come to my inn and refresh yourselves? On the house of course."

We looked at each other and grinned.

"Thank you. That would be most welcome."

We followed him to his small but busy inn and he gave us a table then served us food and drink.

"You are a very generous man. What is your name?"

He chuckled and said "Isaac but my friends call me Bubba."

"Then Bubba we'll tell all our friends about your inn and your welcome and hope this does some good for your business."

He grinned widely and thanked us, then went about his business. As we finished our superb dinner, I went to thank Bubba personally.

"Bubba. Thank you once again for your hospitality and I hope we will meet again someday."

He grabbed my hand and shook it.

"It was my privilege to have you in my home. You are welcome here any time. And if you need somewhere to stay, I have a friend at the other end of the village, whom I'm sure will gladly put you up. Actually, there is a wedding happening there in the next few days. Maybe you could go – I'm sure that they would all welcome you."

I seemed to remember having relatives in Cana.

"What is your friend's name?" I asked.

"His name is Joseph. Joseph of Arimathea."

"Thank you once again, Bubba."

"You're welcome."

He turned and carried on serving his customers with infectious jollity.

I turned to Peter.

"Do you know, I'm sure I have an Uncle Joseph in Cana. Do you think anyone would object if we went to see him and attend the wedding?"

"Jesus, we all would follow you to the ends of the Earth. I'm sure going to a wedding in this town won't be a problem. Let's get back to camp and see what the others have to say?"

We were the last to arrive back at the camp. As we sat for our evening meal and went over the day's events, I spoke about Bubba and the upcoming wedding.

"Would anybody object to going to a wedding?"

All looked around, nodding. Peter just looked at me and said, "Told you so!"

"I do believe that it may be a wedding of a relative of mine. I have a vague recollection of an Uncle Joseph who I've not seen since I was a child."

It was decided we would go. The next day we packed up and headed out for the far end of Cana where the wedding was being held. Bubba had given us clear directions and we soon reached our destination. There was a shepherd in a field and I decided to check we were in the right place.

"Hello. Could you tell me if this is the home of Joseph?"

"Yes. This is his farm and I am his son. Who are you?"

His gaze was wary.

"My name is Jesus of Nazareth and I've come with my friends to join a wedding hosted by a man called Joseph, who I think is my uncle?"

He looked me up and down then glanced over at my friends.

"Well, you have certainly come to the right place Jesus and yes, there is a wedding here and yes, it is one of your relatives."

"Well, it is lucky that we will be here to witness it."

I was excited that I would be meeting more of my family.

"You do know that your mother is coming?" the shepherd added.

I was amazed.

"My mother?"

"She is travelling and should be arriving at any time now. If you want somewhere to stay, the barn is free or you can pitch up beside it. It's up to you. Sorry, I can't stay to chat but I'll see you later."

And with that walked off further into the field with his sheep following.

It was true, the wedding was to be here at Joseph's home. I was so eager to see my mother as we hadn't seen each other for a long time.

We decided to camp down in the shelter of the barn. Once we had sorted our things out, we sat outside, where we had a view of the town.

It didn't seem that long before we could see a group of people trudging through the town in our direction.

Somehow, I knew my mother was amongst these people and got up and made my way towards them.

As I got closer, I searched the faces of the women for a familiar face. It wasn't easy as all their faces were covered with shawls to protect them against the dust of the desert. I couldn't see my mother and I felt deflated.

Then a small group was coming up at the back of the main crowd. It was obvious they were trying to keep up. I searched faces again and sure enough, there she was looking all dishevelled and dusty. She was carrying a linen package on her head of now silver hair.

I stopped as I wanted to watch her without her realising I was there. But in the end, I couldn't contain myself.

"Mother."

Every woman looked at me. It hadn't occurred to me that practically all the women would be known as Mother to someone!

I shouted again, using her name.

"Mary. Mary."

My mother stopped and looked at me through squinted eyes with a hand over to provide shade from the sun's glare. Her face told me she didn't quite recognise my voice.

"Who calls me?"

I started to feel a little queasy in my stomach as I moved towards her. She still didn't recognise me. Pushing my long hair back and scraping my beard to a neat point, I went to her.

"It's me, Mother. Jesus, your son."

There was a moment that seemed to last almost forever. She stared at me, rubbed her eyes and let the bundle she was skilfully balancing on her head drop to the floor. She clasped her hands to her mouth and wept freely.

"Jesus. My son. Is it really you?"

We stood opposite each other, a few inches apart. I was now a tall 32-year-old man. She was still the mother I had always known but now she seemed smaller. She had to look up to meet my eyes; it used to be the other way around. The dust did nothing to hide her beautiful face and time had not won the battle on her skin. When she smiled, my heart skipped a beat. She fell forwards into my arms and flung hers around me burying her face in my chest.

"Oh, my son. My wonderful son."

She sobbed as she looked up at me.

"How I have missed you. Every day I would watch the path up to the house to see if you were coming and prayed that you would come home. I have heard about your travels and I prayed that you were safe from harm."

I smiled down at this wonderful woman and searched her face that I have kept in my heart.

"There has not been one day that I have not thought about you too. I am sorry for not coming home more often but I am on God's mission. It has taken me throughout the land and I have walked many miles and met some wonderful people. But none so wonderful as you, my mother."

I hugged her close and realised that all the others had gone and we were alone in the middle of the street.

"Come, you must be tired. Let me take your things."

I picked up her bundle, put my arm around her

shoulders and we walked to the house where she was staying with her relatives. They were waiting at the door for her to arrive and were happy to see her as we entered. I put the bundle on the floor and helped Mother to a chair.

Uncle Joseph came over with a cup of water.

"Here Mary, have some water. You must be thirsty after your long journey? Are you hungry?"

She shook her head and drank all the water. When she took the last few drops from the cup, she closed her eyes and sighed.

"Thank you Joseph for your hospitality. You have made me feel so welcome."

She stood up and came over to me and looked straight into my eyes then turned to Joseph.

"I would like to introduce you to my son. This is Jesus and Jesus, this is your Uncle Joseph."

He came to me, put his arms on my shoulders and kissed both my cheeks.

"Welcome Jesus, it has been a long time since we last met. You may not remember me as you were a small child when we last met and here you are now a grown man."

I searched his face and although I'd had a vague recollection of a previous meeting when I was younger, I could not remember that face. But I liked him immediately.

Mother was looking tired now and wanted to go to sleep. Uncle Joseph showed her to her cot and we all wished each other good night.

I left to go back to the barn to my companions. They too were getting ready for the night and asked me how I had got on. I looked around at their expectant faces and just smiled. They knew what it meant and didn't need to say anything.

The following day was when the wedding was to be held. All the guests were helping out with various tasks – this was our way. The whole place was buzzing with activity; it was like a beehive. We helped out by putting hay bales into a big circle for the guests to sit on. Thanks to my father for my carpentry skills, I made an altar canopy, over which we tied some linen, to help keep the sun off the happy couple and the Rabbi whilst the service was being carried out.

It was a wonderful service. I had never been to a wedding before and neither had some of my companions. My cousin looked beautiful with flowers in her long hair and her betrothed was scrubbed clean and his hair combed. His beard was beginning to show as he was turning into a young man.

The women had prepared a wonderful wedding feast and laid it out on the long table made from planks of wood resting on boxes and an old gate. There was plenty of food for everyone. There was wine which I hadn't tasted for a while. Everyone was relaxed and enjoying the dancing and singing.

It was wonderful to be part of this celebration as we had been travelling for what seemed like an age; we needed this rest and time to collect ourselves.

Mother came to me with a concerned look on her face.

"Mother, what's wrong?"

"Nothing for you to worry about Jesus. Just a little embarrassment for the family, that's all," she said quietly.

"Is there anything I can do to help?" I offered.

"I don't think so. It's the wine — there is very little left as more people have come to witness the marriage than planned and everyone is enjoying Uncle Joseph's hospitality. He doesn't know what to do and is now feeling ashamed. I know that you have helped others in their need. Is there anything you can do to help? Joseph will not ask you himself."

I knew what she was asking me to do and I argued with myself about it.

Surely I couldn't ask God for help such as this?

Surely this would have been an abuse of his power to do this?

What would the wedding guests think?

Would they think it wrong; would they realise I was channelling God's power?

I had no idea what to do, so I asked the disciples and they all agreed that I should do this because sooner or later, everyone would start to accept that God's power existed.

"I'll do it then. Mother, will you take me to the area where the casks are please?"

She grabbed my hand and we all made our way through the happy, dancing crowd, who had no idea what I was about to do.

We arrived to see Uncle carefully measuring out the last drops of wine into the clay jugs. He looked up at me, then Mother.

"What are we to do — this is the last."

Joseph was a proud and generous man, always helping those who needed it, sharing his crops with those who had none. This made what I was about to do easier to bear.

"Uncle, please have your servants fill the casks with fresh water."

Uncle Joseph looked at Mother and she nodded approval. The servants quickly filled the casks with water from the well until they were all full. All eyes were fixed on me, barely blinking.

I had to do this now and said to Mother, "It is too soon yet for others to see this Mother but I do this for you."

I raised my hands, closed my eyes and whispered to God, "I do this in your name. Not for personal gain but so that it may help in my quest to spread the word of the way. I thank you."

I dropped my hands and filled a cup from the cask and passed it to Joseph.

"Here Uncle, taste it for me please."

He received it with a look of doubt on his face but as he looked into it, the doubt turned to astonishment. It was dark red instead of clear water. Then he tasted the liquid. The cup fell from his hand spilling the contents on the floor. All watching saw that it was wine that ran on the sandy floor, staining it red. The servants stood, eyes wide and mouths open.

The place was silent until Uncle Joseph broke in saying "Here, fill your jugs quickly and take it to the people."

The servants filled the jugs and ran into the crowd of wedding guests, each oblivious as to what had just taken place. Then, one man of great stature drank from this new batch and was pleasantly surprised at the taste of the new wine.

"What's this Joseph? Filling us with your basic wine and then serving us with your best. I have never known anybody do that. I commend you, for this is a truly wonderful wine."

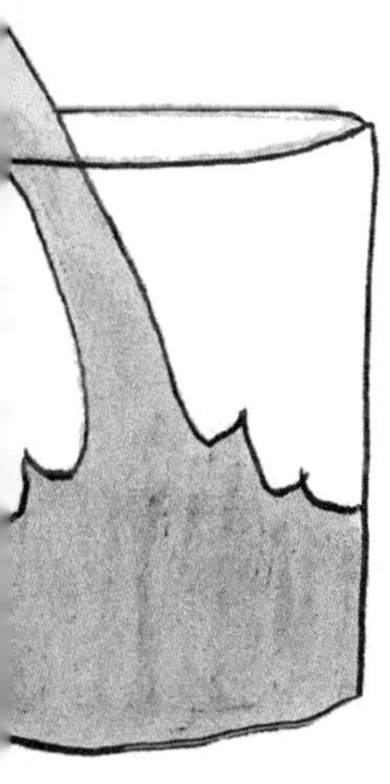

All agreed by raising their cups and filling them again. My uncle sat back on a chair and mopped his brow.

"I don't know what I have just witnessed but it was wonderful."

With a look of disbelief, he took my right hand, shaking it vigorously.

"How can I possibly thank you Jesus? For not only have you saved the day but some of us have witnessed the power of the Lord God through you."

My mother was beside herself with pride.

"Thank you, my son. You have just done a wonderful thing." Then she touched my cheek and smiled looked into my eyes, "Thank you."

We left the next day and I said goodbye to my mother. We both cried and it felt like I would never see her again. I hugged her and didn't want to let her go.

"Be strong son. You have a hard task ahead of you,"

she said with a knowing smile.

"What do you mean Mother?"

She just looked at me and smiled. One more hug and we left.

It was still early as we wanted to avoid the midday sun. We had walked a long way and found ourselves going through a wooded area following the path before us and although we were tired, we were still in good spirits.

Turning a corner, we were met by two men. The bigger of the two had a knife which he waved left to right in front of him. The smaller man stood back with a worried expression on his face. I thought I would try to reason with the armed man but he was not for moving. Then he spoke.

"Valuables. I want your valuables. So don't give me any trouble and no one will get hurt."

He was shaking now and it didn't seem like he had done this before.

"We have no valuables as we travel light but you're welcome to share our bread and water."

I reached over to a bag on the donkey and he panicked.

"Move away from there." Sweat now running down his face. "Just give me your valuables and I… we will be off."

By this time, my disciples had made a circle around the two. The smaller man became very agitated and started grabbing the bigger man's tunic as Matthew moved forward.

"Can't you see you're outnumbered? You don't stand a

chance against us all."

The bigger man lunged forward at Matthew but he was nimble and moved out of the way and, as he turned, caught the robber on the head with his staff. The robber, dazed, stood upright and made another swipe at Matthew, this time catching him in the chest, making him drop his staff.

The robber went in again and as he did, the rest of my disciples made a dash for him, grabbed his hair and tunic pulling him backwards. The knife flew out of his hands as he tried to defend himself but he was overpowered. The smaller robber just gave in and fell to his knees sobbing.

"I didn't want to do this, it was his idea," he sobbed.

Matthew was lying against a tree holding his wound, bright red blood was trickling down his tunic. I went to him and he looked up.

"I'll be fine. I'm usually a quick healer," he jested.

I could see by the blood flow that it was more than a scratch. I looked back at the men who were holding the bigger captive and were tying him to a tree with rope.

"See what you've done," said the smaller. "Now we shall lose our lives and for what? Nothing. I knew I should never have come. Please forgive my sin. What can I do to make it up to you? I'm not a bad man. I am a peaceful God-loving man."

And he sobbed more.

I looked back at Matthew. His eyes were beginning to close and he was slumped against the tree. I felt now that I must ask God for help, so I raised my hands closed my eyes.

"Oh Heavenly Father, I need your help."

I looked up to the sky. I felt a glow over my body and warmth in my right hand. I looked down at Matthew and touched his shoulder believing...

Believing.

I closed my eyes and thought of Matthew. There was silence until Matthew broke it with a cough. I opened my eyes. The blood had stopped the wound healed and Matthew was staring at me.

The men fell to their knees. They had followed me on the strength of the stories. Now they had witnessed the true power of the Lord God.

Matthew slowly stood up and moved his arm up and down, left and right and then he too went down on his knees.

"You have taken me into your family. You have given me purpose. Now you have given me my life. How can I possibly thank you? There are no words."

I looked down at his glowing face and realised that he was now with God.

"Rise up Matthew, for you have been reborn and your new life begins now. I have helped show you the way but it was Lord God who gave you back your life. Give thanks and praise to him as much as you can and spread the word so that all can share in your new-found happiness."

He rose up and went straight to the bigger of the two robbers and untied him. Standing back he said, "See what you have just witnessed. Does it make you sad to see the life you have chosen? I have set you free as I understand there is good in all men. Prove me right and we will let you go."

The men stared on in amazement at Matthew's

new- found faith and the fact that he had just released the man who nearly killed him.

"Do you wish to go or would you like to stay and make a better person of yourself?"

The bigger man looked around; everyone was still and silent. He looked over to his companion and he was also quiet but nodding to influence him. This time the bigger man went to his knees.

"I am truly sorry Matthew. I had lost my way and didn't know what else to do. I persuaded Thomas that we should try this. Please forgive me," he pleaded.

I looked at the bigger man and although he seemed true, his eyes had a coldness.

"What is your name?"

"I am Judas. Judas Iscariot. I am your servant."

"Well Judas Iscariot, if your intentions are genuine we welcome you to our brethren."

He looked up nodding profusely, wringing his hands together, looking around at the other faces. He stood and went to Thomas with bowed head and asked for forgiveness. Thomas accepted.

Whilst I accepted this man into the fold, there was something about him; I was honestly not sure about this fellow.

We started back on our journey with two new companions. One by one the men came to walk beside me to talk about the new members of our group but especially Judas.

Did we trust him?

Why did you let him join us?

Would we have to sleep with one eye open?

My response to each question was the same, "Let he without sin cast the first stone."

This eased their minds.

So now we were thirteen, travelling to the Mount: Peter; Andrew; James; John; Bartholomew; James; Thaddeus; Matthew, Judas; Thomas; Simon and Philip. Our bond was good.

It was slow going to the Mount but we were all in high spirits and became good friends. Judas clung to my every word and became my shadow. I think he just needed structure and a cause. I hoped he had found that through me.

Thomas had settled in well but when we told stories, he questioned if they were truthful and had moments of doubt. He quickly became known as doubting Thomas, which he hated but it was all in good fun. Soon though, his doubting would be put to the test.

We needed to fill our water bags and found a stream. As we approached the stream, we came across a leper who was camped out there. The group immediately held back in fear, as lepers were considered the most unclean of all people – they were outcasts. It was up to me to approach him and as I did, the man recoiled away in shame as my friends looked on. He tried to stand, which caused him agonising pain and instantly my heart went to him.

"What is your name friend?" I asked, trying to gain his confidence.

He mumbled, "Joseph," and coughed profusely.

I helped him to sit back down and sat with him.

"What are you doing? Have you come to mock me as most do?"

I couldn't see his face properly. Like his body, it was mostly covered with dirty cloths. He smelled terrible.

"No Joseph, I would like to help you."

"Help me? How can you possibly help me? I am wretched. I am cast out. I am a lost soul. The only way you can help me is by slitting my throat. I would end it myself but I cannot. I live here amongst the trees listening to the birds, drinking from the glittering stream and smelling the flowers and the herbs that grow wild here. How can I die when I have all this?"

He slumped down and began to weep. Despite his condition, he still marvelled at his surroundings.

"You still have the will to live, don't you? With God's creations all around?"

I tried desperately to console him but he was angry.

"God? If there only was such a person, then surely he wouldn't let me live like this, would he?"

I could see now that, although he appreciated what he had, his faith had truly gone. He was blinded by his terrible fate and I needed to renew his faith.

I asked him to stand.

"I have listened to you and I think I can help but you must trust me."

"What have I got to lose. I am already a dead man walking. I can go no lower. Do your worst."

By this time, the others had gathered around and watched intently, especially Thomas, whose face looked troubled and disbelieving.

I held Joseph by the arm. "Joseph was my father's name. I shall bless you on his behalf. We shall go into the water, so do not be afraid."

He cowered at the thought, so I smiled and said "I shall not force you to go. You must want to go of your own free will."

Reluctantly, he took small painful steps forward and stopped.

"I am scared. What am I to do if I cannot get out?"

Don't worry, I will guide you and if we falter, the others will come to our aid. Put your trust in me and think of God helping you. Ready?"

He nodded and we slowly made our way into the cool stream which shone in the sun. As we got further into the water, his stature started to change and I felt strength come to his arm. When the water reached our chests, I stopped him.

"Are you ready?"

He hesitated and nodded.

"I am going to baptise you in this water so that you are ready to receive faith in the Lord God our father."

"Okay, okay just get on with it."

Joseph was scared and desperate, but willing; after all, he had become lost and needed guidance.

I held his hand and his head.

"On my command, fall back into the water. Have no fear as I shall be your guide. My arms will be there to catch you and help you back up. I will say the words and you will then fall, are you okay with that?"

He didn't answer, so I began.

"I baptise thee in the name of God our father."

Then I dropped him backwards so he went into the water. He didn't struggle or panic and when I helped him up, he came up with ease.

"Are you okay?"

Spluttering he said, "Yes I am and I am still alive. At first, I thought you were trying to drown me but I had a calm sensation enter my soul and it felt good."

We made our way out of the water and everyone came down to help. Joseph was standing more upright and I noticed that his walking was less laboured.

"I feel different," he exclaimed.

"You have become one with God. Now you are not lost and I have helped you find your way. God has granted you new life through me."

His wet rags were beginning to fall from his body and he started to unwrap them from his head. The other men looked on. Joseph's long straggly hair fell down and his face beamed through his beard. His hands slowly went to his face and felt the contours of his skin. He started laughing and babbling with excitement.

"What have you done?" he questioned. "I have become a whole man again."

He looked down at his fingers. They were no longer gnarled and broken but long and slender. He inspected both sides top, back, top, back and each time he laughed. Then suddenly he stopped and looked at me.

"I dare not take the rest of my wrappings off."

I smiled at him and put my arms out and replied, "You have been blessed. Do not fear for God is with you and within you, so go ahead."

He looked bewildered as he stared down at his rag wrapped body and began to tear and rip them away, revealing a skinny, yet whole body. By this time, the men were all on their knees, even Thomas, who clearly had no more doubts.

Joseph stood there crying and laughing at the same time. Tears of joy were streaming down his healed face and his feet were able to kick the sand on the bank. He too went down on his knees unable to keep in his emotions inside.

"Thank you, Lord. Thank you, Lord," he cried, over and over.

I went to him with a robe I had taken from one of the bags on the donkey and handed it to him.

"Here, you will need to get dressed. Now you can discard your rags and dress like a man."

He reluctantly held out his hands and I placed the robe over them. He held it out in front of him and inspected it. Front and back and slowly hugging it to himself, squeezing it with every ounce of love that he had.

He looked me in the eyes, "Today is the start of a new day. Not only have you made me a man but I have also found God again. I shall go out into the world with my head held high and everywhere I go I shall preach the word of the Lord." He held the garment up to the sky. "Praise be to you our Lord for today I have been reborn."

Joseph pulled the garment over his head and stood there as proud and strong as any man.

"God be with you, my friend," he said.

"God be with you too Joseph."

We had found another sheep and this one would roam the land spreading the word.

"Before you go Master, what is your name so that I can tell the world of you and this wonderful day?"

"Jesus. Jesus of Nazareth."

"Then Jesus of Nazareth, I shall make it my new life's work to go out into the world and tell everyone how you helped me find God and myself. I shall go to the synagogues to listen and learn and then spread the word. For now, I am a new man."

He cried and laughed all at the same time, muttering to himself, looking at his hands and feet with wonder. We left him with our hearts and our faith even stronger.

⸺

After leaving Joseph at the stream to make his own way, we soon arrived at the Mount. There were many gathered there already. My disciples and I made our way to the top where we sat down and looked around at the multitudes.

Judas said, "There are many here for you Jesus. All have come to hear you speak the word of the Lord."

Judas had become a good friend. As we travelled, he would stay by my side and help me at any point and our bond grew stronger.

"I think it's time. I shall make my way to the point." As I walked forward my companions clapped and shouted to attract the crowd's attention.

I looked around at all the expectant faces waiting for

me to speak. I didn't know where to start but I need not have worried as the words just spilt out of my mouth like torrential rain. Then I blessed them and praised them.

By the time I had finished, I was exhausted but felt proud and blessed. With the disciples' help, I made my way into the crowds, giving a blessing as I met each person. I couldn't believe the response and how the word of the Lord was being spread.

Soon darkness started to fall and the people began to disperse. We hadn't expected so many people and it was very overwhelming.

CHAPTER 10

32

Life around Judea was very civil. The Romans were keeping law and order and, as long as you stayed out of trouble, you were left alone.

Unfortunately, because of my outburst at the temple with the moneylenders, I had drawn the attention of the new King, Herod Antipas. He was named after his father Herod the Great and was just like him. He didn't like that people had started calling me the 'King of the Jews'. To be honest, I didn't like this title either as it was not true – I was just the messenger of God trying to spread his word. Herod was having none of it and felt threatened. We had to be careful in many towns and villages as the guards would provoke and threaten us.

Then, one day the devastating news about my beloved John was brought to us. John had told Herod not to marry his brother Philip's wife as this was not approved of by our God. In his anger, Herod imprisoned John. His new bride,

Herodias, hated John for what he had said. For Herod to prove his love for Herodias, she demanded John's head on a plate. Herod was only too happy to comply.

I was sick to my soul when I heard the news; I couldn't believe what had happened. Once the news had become public, a period of mourning fell across the land. This didn't help matters either as Herod was becoming more and more unstable – he saw everything as a threat to his power.

I didn't know how to respond to questions about why had God not helped John. I needed to be alone to try to come to terms with this. I told the disciples that I needed time and, although all were sad in their hearts, they all agreed to my request. They knew it was not for me but for John; to each of us, he was a foundation in our belief.

I made my way down to the water's edge and asked one of the fishermen if I could use his small boat so that I could sail over to the desert on the other side of the water. The fisherman gladly agreed and I set off for the other side. There was still enough daylight for me to navigate and I aimed for the hill on the land opposite. When I landed, there was a large group of people camped along the water's edge.

I got out of the little boat, one of them recognised me.

"It's Jesus, look, there in the boat. It's the Lamb of God."

They crowded around me, touching my shoulders, arms and hair. I must admit I felt very intimidated as more and more people appeared from the shore. Then, noticing my discomfort, a few of the men circled me to give me space.

There were a few scuffles but no one was hurt. I forgot my own anguish as those who were afflicted and desperate called for my help. I took pity on them by healing the sick and infirm.

The group of men helping me tried to disperse the crowd but to no avail. The crowd knew who I was and wanted to be near me and hear my words. So I asked them to sit and I would talk to them. Like a wave, the request to sit down passed through the crowd until there was a mass of faces looking at me expectantly.

When I had finished speaking, I told them to go about their daily chores and to go feed themselves.

A woman shouted, "How can we Lord? This is the desert and we have come to you unprepared without provisions."

I looked at the men, "Have they nothing?"

Then a young boy called out from the crowd.

"I have five loaves of bread and two fish if that helps."

I asked the young boy to come forward with his provisions and he laid his basket in front of me. I put my hand on his head, blessed him and thanked him.

"Now that you have given it willingly, this is enough treasure for all."

He smiled and went back to his mother. I looked over to the five men who had helped organise the crowd and asked them to bring me as many baskets as they could find and put them side-by-side.

There was a frenzy of activity as they looked for baskets and it wasn't long before there was a row of baskets lined up along the water's edge.

I lifted my arms and closed my eyes to speak to the

heavens. I gave thanks to my Lord God.

Then I said to the first man, "Take these loaves of bread and fish to the baskets and fill them."

He hesitated and looked at his friends who pushed him forward. He came over to me and I gave him the offerings. Looking down at the two fish and five loaves, then looking back at his friends, he shrugged his shoulders and went to the first basket and threw in a loaf. Then the second and the third and so on, until he had put one in each basket.

"Come, take the baskets and feed the people."

The other four men came to the baskets and gasped in amazement.

"They are full. They are all full!" said one.

They each took a basket and began to feed the multitudes. I watched as the baskets emptied and refilled, emptied and refilled until everyone was fed.

Some of my disciples had sailed over the water to make sure I was okay as they knew I was upset about John. They were surprised to see what was going on. As they landed, they saw all the joyous people. Peter saw me first and came over. He had a puzzled look on his face.

"Jesus. What is happening? Why are all these people here?"

I put my arms out to welcome him and we embraced.

"Welcome, Peter. These people have just witnessed God's power through me. There were sick and infirm people I had to help and then they all needed feeding."

Peter listened intently and looked over to the baskets still brimming with fish and bread.

"Master, tell me what happened. Where did all this food come from? How is this possible?"

"I asked God for help," I replied.

He stared at me with a look of amazement and said, "So, are you okay? I know how much you loved John."

His concern touched me and I told him, "All is well. You can return across the water but I'm going to go to the Mount and pray for John. There's no need to wait for me, I'll come back to you soon."

There was little daylight left and it looked as if a storm was coming. Big black clouds were beginning to form over the sea. I didn't want to stay on the Mount all night and made my way up as quickly as I could. I clambered up the side of the mount and followed a path made by a goat along the edge until I found a rock to sit on.

I looked up to the sky and studied the clouds for a moment when a familiar scent wafted towards me from the sea.

"Nana," I whispered and sure enough, there she was.

"Oh Nana, how I have missed you."

I stood to greet her.

"Hello, my boy. You seem to be coping well with all

that is being thrown at you."

I sat back down. I was weary, tired and hungry. My face was lined with worry.

"But you look terrible. Carrying the weight of the world on your shoulders isn't easy, is it?"

She came forward as if to hug me but of course, she could not.

"Some days I do struggle, Nana," I sighed. "Just when I think things are going well, another problem bears its ugly fangs and I'm back to the beginning."

She came to my side and stared out at the vast desert.

"When you look out, what do you see?"

I followed the direction she was looking at.

"I see desert, sand and a stormy sky. I see trees and bushes – a vast expanse of nothing."

My heart was heavy thinking of John and how I would never see him again until we met in heaven.

"Look again. This time look with your heart, not with your eyes."

I closed my eyes and there was John, smiling at me. I remembered all the things we did when we were children, when we parted and how wonderful it was when we met on the River Jordan. Then I recalled when he baptised me. My heart began to lighten and a smile came to my face.

"What do you see now Jesus?" Nana asked.

"I see many things. Many wonderful things. My life has been truly blessed."

I was feeling lifted again.

"So you see Jesus, it's not always what you see with your eyes, it's also what you see with your heart."

I stood there looking out to the desert smiling to

myself. When I turned, Nana had gone.

I was becoming accustomed to her coming and going. I accepted the fact that she would just go without saying goodbye.

⁂

The storm was now picking up and the wind was beginning to howl around the Mount. I decided to make my way back to the shore and go home. The time was right as I was feeling stronger after seeing Nana again.

When I reached the shore, everyone had left as I had instructed them. The little boat that I borrowed from the fisherman was still there. I pushed it into the sea and started to row. The storm was now picking up pace and as I got further out on the water, I could hear loud voices shouting in fear. My rowing became laboured. I listened and was sure that it was Peter's voice shouting. I called out loudly over the storm.

"Peter. Peter. Is that you?"

A distant voice came back.

"Yes Jesus. Where are you?"

I followed the direction the voice was coming from, rowing harder and harder. I could just make out the shape of their boat in the darkness.

"Peter. I am here to your left."

The rain beat down heavily, which made it hard to see but I battled on regardless. Then with a thump, I had hit the side of their boat and it started taking on water as the waves got higher and higher.

Without thinking, I raised my hands and spoke to the Lord, hoping that he would grant my wish. I was about to test my own faith.

As the boat took on more water and was closer to sinking, I stepped over the side, holding my hands aloft.

I was standing on the water.

Slowly I started to walk towards Peter. I was walking on the water.

"Peter. Peter, can you hear me?" I shouted.

"Yes Master, we can hear you but still can't see you," he cried.

As Nana had taught me, this was another test of faith.

"Look with your heart Peter as well as your eyes."

I was standing in front of their boat and could see Peter holding onto the side with one hand, shielding his eyes with the other from the torrential rain. Then they saw me.

The sea around me was calm, yet their boat was being tossed around the water like a salmon being landed amongst a huge catch.

"Surely this is not true. How can a man walk on water?" one man asked.

"But this is no ordinary man. This is the Lamb of God."

Peter began to climb over the side of his boat.

"I want to help you Jesus. Let me walk on the water too." He started to walk but the waves lashed him hard and he doubted his faith and began to sink into the water.

"Help me Master… please, I am sinking."

I was close enough now, so I reached out and helped

him up and the others pulled him back to safety.

"Why did I sink master?" He was distraught.

"Your faith was strong until it was tested, Peter. When the waves challenged you, your faith faltered and you sank."

I was still on the water and needed to calm the storm. Once again, I raised my hands and asked it to be calm. Gradually, the storm receded until we were floating on a now tranquil sea. The men looked all around and dared not let go of the sides of the boat. I was still standing on the water in front of them.

"Truly, you have God's mercy. How can we ever disbelieve you?"

I walked to the boat and they helped me in. Then, when we were all settled, they gave thanks to God.

CHAPTER 11

33

The killing of John had made us realise that we were in great danger from Herod. Not only that, but this act caused panic amongst the people. They no longer trusted or liked Herod. There was tension between the Rabbis and priests about the stories that we were telling.

As we travelled, our stories had become more elaborate and at times it was hard to believe some of them ourselves they were so fantastical.

I had a childhood friend named Lazarus and the story about to unfold about him was almost way beyond belief too.

I hadn't seen Lazarus for a good while but heard that he wasn't well. I didn't realise that his illness was so serious until news reached me that he had died. Lazarus' had lived with his two sisters in their home four days away in Bethany. I felt that I must go and comfort his sisters.

The journey was uneventful and on arrival, we were greeted by a group of mourners. I asked where the sisters were and was told they were at Lazarus' tomb. My companions agreed I should go to the tomb alone. A couple of other mourners offered to show me the way even though it wasn't far.

The tomb was set in a chamber in the rock and sealed with a large stone, as was usual. Lazarus had been interred in the chamber tomb for four days, anointed with precious oils and wrapped in clean white cloth.

Mary, her sister Martha and a few mourners were knelt next to the stone door, weeping and praying for Lazarus.

When they saw us, some of the women rose to greet us.

Mary couldn't contain herself and flung her arms around me, sobbing.

"Oh Jesus, thank you for coming. It was such a sudden end. One minute he was suffering in bed and the next, he'd gone."

"I don't know what to say Mary. Had I known he was so ill, I would have come sooner."

Their grief poured out. I offered comfort to both Mary and Martha. I felt dreadful that as a man with a reputation for healing the sick, I had not been there to help my old friend and now it was simply too late as he had been dead for four days. Tears began to fill my eyes.

Was it too late to ask my Lord for help after four days? Surely I had no choice but to try to help my friends and family in the same way I helped strangers? But, helping Uncle Joseph with wine was one thing – this was a different matter altogether.

"Mary, Martha, could you get some help to move the stone to open the tomb?"

"Why Jesus? There will be the dreadful stench of death. What good can you do – it's too late?"

"Please, do as I ask."

The sisters rounded up as many men as they could and as they started to move the huge stone, I once again looked to the heavens to begin my prayer to God.

"Oh Father, if you can hear me, I beg you, release Lazarus from the clutches of death and bring him back to us unharmed and well. I ask this not for myself but for my dear friend and his family."

I closed my eyes and wept. This was

going to be the biggest thing I had ever asked of God. I went to the opening of the tomb and stood in prayer.

Then I shouted out, "Lazarus, awaken and come out. Come back to us. If you hear me, please make it known."

It was silent and all eyes fixed on the tomb entrance. Then a glow appeared from within and a voice broke the silence.

"Mary… Mary… Help me, I can't move."

Whispers of disbelief rang around and all stayed still.

"Mary, Martha, please help me. I am bound and cannot move. Can you hear me?"

Martha fell to the floor faint. A few came to her help her but dare not go too near the tomb.

Mary looked at me. I smiled.

"Go to Lazarus Mary; he needs your help. Do not be afraid. He will be as you knew him before but still wrapped in his burial cloths and unable to move."

Mary, filled with trepidation, smiled weakly back at me and looked over to the tomb entrance where the glow was coming from. Slowly, she approached. I followed her to show support and we stood close to the entrance. Mary looked back at me, still unsure. I waved her on encouragingly. The other mourners began to move closer. This made Mary braver, knowing there was support, and finally, she entered the tomb.

"Ohh… ohh… my Lazarus… my Lazarus."

The crowd were shocked and afraid to hear the voice of Lazarus coming from the tomb. They retreated further back to where there was more shelter and watched on in amazement.

Mary went further into the tomb and Lazarus turned

his head to her and said "Mary, please help me. I need water; I am so thirsty."

Scared, she went to him with a water bag and aimed it at his dry cracked lips, pouring some of the water over him.

"Mary, untie me so that I can hold you. I'm scared and do not know what is happening to me. Where am I?" His eyes were darting all around. Mary dropped the water bag and tried desperately to untie the wrappings. As she did so, he began to move his arms and helped with the rest until he sat there naked. Mary stood and put her hands over her mouth in disbelief, staring down at her previously dead brother.

"How do you feel Lazarus?" she asked. "You have been brought back from the dead by Jesus."

Lazarus looked up in shock.

"But how is this possible? How can I be dead one moment and alive the next?"

Mary went to him, held him under his arm and gently helped him to his feet.

"Come on brother, let's not question this miracle but go out and give praise to Jesus and God, for it is them who we have to thank."

He looked at her, smiled and nodded as they made their way to the entrance. Outside, a crowd had gathered. Many had gone to the town declaring that a miracle had happened. All were now there waiting in silence, eyes wide open, not blinking in case they missed something. Mary came out into the bright sunlight shielding her eyes with one hand and helping Lazarus with the other. I went forward to help.

People wailed, wept and clapped; a cacophony of noise filled the air. There was doubt and disbelief in everyone's eyes but they couldn't stop watching. Most fell to their knees. Some at the back were scared and suspicious, saying this must be the work of the devil. These were non-believers and they threw stones as we came out but were stopped by the others.

Then Lazarus came out into the mayhem as if reborn. He was as naked as his first day on Earth as he slowly made his way out with Mary as support. By this time, Martha had recovered from her faint and ran up to them laughing with delight and giving praise to God. She took over from me and the two sisters helped their brother to a rock nearby where he could sit. Somebody brought a robe for him and slipped it over his head. Another brought more water but all who came close were scared and quickly retreated. By this time, virtually the whole townspeople were somewhere nearby.

The elders had heard what had happened and instead of embracing the miracle, shunned it as being the devil's work. They still had no intention of accepting me for who I was. Although it was a miracle for my friend and his family, it was a bad move in the eyes of the Rabbis. It gave them more reason to hate me and try to get rid of me. To them, I was a blasphemer. It's strange that even though we followed the same religion, there was jealousy. They thought that they should have known about the coming of the new Messiah before anyone else. It made them feel unworthy and that their clerical position was being mocked.

Mary, Martha and Lazarus had been helped to their

home and Lazarus was made to lay down and rest. He was so dazed and confused that he kept shaking his head in disbelief. Mary and Martha looked after him. Mary took me to one side and held my hand.

"How are we to cope with this miracle Jesus? People will start asking questions and treat us differently."

I thought about it for a few seconds and replied, "Do not worry Mary, I will ask your neighbours to watch over you and Lazarus."

Mary looked at me again but this time there was a look of admiration in her eyes and they glistened with love instead of tears.

"Jesus," she said nervously, "do you think it possible for me to travel with you and your disciples?"

I was taken aback by this question.

"What are you asking Mary?"

She looked deep into my eyes, almost burning into my soul. I felt uncomfortable.

"Mary, you know that I care for you but I cannot commit myself to any other than my Lord God."

I could not give myself to her even though I wanted to. I needed to be free to carry on my mission. Mary looked down, embarrassed.

"I'm sorry I didn't mean to…"

She broke off and I held her hands and kissed her forehead.

"One day Mary. Maybe one day."

My words just left her sad. We both had feelings for each other but I just couldn't have any personal distraction. I was on a mission and had to stay focused.

"You can still travel with us if you like? There is always

room for another and it would be nice to have you near."

She smiled and looked at Martha and Lazarus.

"Go Mary, we will be fine here. I am well enough and we will eagerly wait for your return with wonderful tales of your travels."

Mary looked at me then back to them.

"Thank you. I love you both dearly and today has left a special mark on my heart."

We left Martha and Lazarus to carry on our journey through the deserts, mountains, towns and villages, spreading the good word to all who would listen.

One night while I was sleeping, Nana came to me in a dream. She told me of my destiny.

"Listen carefully Jesus to what I'm going to tell you. You are the chosen one," she sighed. "You have been sent here by our Lord God Almighty to take on the sin of the world. But unfortunately, this will be a heavy burden and your mortal life will come to an abrupt end. All the work you are doing now is laying the foundation for the future of humankind. If they are to survive, you must suffer indignity and die for them. Then you will take on the sin of their world. I shall come one more time to you. When the time comes, you will know.

What you have done and what you do will make you last forever and help make humankind survive. Start to prepare yourself; your future is going to be an unhappy one."

I woke up in a pool of sweat and sat up. Putting my

head in my hands, I started to weep, trying not to wake the others. But one by one they stirred. Judas was the first to wake.

"What troubles you Master?"

The others looked on, some rubbed their eyes and yawned. I composed myself and began.

"It has been prophesied that I have been chosen to save humankind from itself. All of my life's work has been for this ending. We are to expect trouble coming and must stay strong through it all by keeping the faith."

I looked down, saddened by what Nana had told me.

"Then we shall get through this together. We shall stay by your side no matter what. Our faith in you and God is limitless."

"Thank you, my friends. I am sorry if it has been hard for you – all the travelling and now this unrest with the Romans. We must fight the good fight. Stay together and stay strong, no matter what."

There was a feeling of unrest amongst the disciples but all were still eager to carry on.

"Maybe it was just a bad dream Master? I have them all the time," said Judas laughing.

The next day, to lighten our mood, we decided to go into Jerusalem and get amongst the people. We were on the move once more. I gave a short sermon before we left to strengthen our spirits and then we were off; three donkeys, twelve disciples, a few women and me. We had decided to let some women come with us as – all were welcome on our journey. They travelled with us for the spiritual journey and not one that would include the pleasures of the flesh. This made it easy for us to become a new family for each other – especially as many had left their own families behind.

The desert was its usual unforgiving self but we had endured it time and again, so we knew what we were dealing with, how to walk across it even in our sandals, and how to cope with the searing heat.

As we drew closer to the city, we could see there were many people about within the gates. When they realised who we were, they ran towards the city gates.

"He is here… he is here. The King of the Jews has come!"

We could see through the gates that people started to put palm leaves on the floor.

"Jesus, I think you should ride donkey into the city. It will be a sign to the people that you are the one they seek," advised Peter.

It seemed like the right thing to do, although I was reluctant to make a fuss. So, I mounted a donkey to ride through the gates and into the city. As we moved along the streets, we were met by throngs of people laying palms before us, singing and praising the Lord, calling out above the noise.

"Hail Jesus. King of the Jews."

"Why do they call me King of the Jews? I make no claim to that?"

The Roman guards watched with contempt. You could tell they were hoping for trouble to make their day more interesting.

The Rabbis at the synagogue were looking on in disgust from the doorway, as we were now becoming more of a threat to them and their teachings. They turned and filed their way back inside so they were not forced to meet with us.

We pulled up to the Market Square, I got off the donkey and thanked him for carrying me by rubbing his ears and feeding him a carrot which he gladly crunched on. There was a small raised area in the square where groups would perform plays and songs. It looked like a fine place to talk to the people. I was helped onto the platform and we joined in hushing the crowd. When all was quiet, I began talking about the way, how things should be and what to expect from each other. I remembered the words that Nana said last time she came to me – how I would have to die to save them all. This spurred me on to give a powerful sermon on making sure we lived, not just survived.

Just as the crowds were beginning to listen and concentrate on my words, the Rabbis came over with Roman guards and told me to stop speaking or I would be arrested. The crowd jeered and scolded and insisted that I was allowed to carry on. I knew what the consequences would be but, to the anger of the Rabbis, I still carried on.

"Guards. Arrest that man."

It was obvious that the Romans would take great pleasure in this particular duty, as they pushed through the crowds. They grabbed me and I didn't try to get free; I knew then that this was all part of the plan that Nana had told me about.

The crowd jeered and shouted and threw their palm

leaves at the guards. The disciples wanted to retaliate and help me escape. But I was calm about what was happening.

"Do not trouble yourself, for I will have God with me."

The guards dragged me through the angry mobs into the synagogue and made me kneel before the Rabbis. They stood as if regal and holy, but really, they were neither; I could see that now.

"So… you say you are the Messiah. King of the Jews. Son of God?" pronounced the elder Rabbi.

I looked up at them all.

"You say I am. Not I."

I chose not to argue but remained calm.

"Do not be clever with me or I shall have you flogged. Now, are you or are you not the Messiah?"

Once again, I looked up at this Rabbi.

"I have never declared that I am. But I am the son of God as we all are. God is father to all."

They turned their backs on me and formed a huddle to talk about me. Then the elder turned back to face me.

"Your answer is fair and clever, and we have no proof to be able to hold you. But mark my words, we will be watching you and if you continue this blasphemy, you will leave us no other alternative. Now leave and take heed of my words."

The guards, disappointed, pulled me roughly to my feet and turned me into the street. There, at the bottom of the steps, were my disciples.

"Praise be to God," they shouted. "We were certain that we would never see you again."

We left the centre of Jerusalem quickly and went to a garden called Gethsemane on the Mount of Olives. It was fragrant with the scent of the olive trees and overlooked the valley beside Jerusalem. Here we made a campfire and slept under the stars.

This night was to be the last visit from Nana. As I slept, she came to me.

"Wake up Jesus. Go to the rock across the garden, I must speak with you."

Instantly I woke up and looked around at the others. All were snoring peacefully. I rose quietly and made my way over to the rock that Nana had told me to go and waited. The night was cool and the soft breeze ran little rings of leaves around the olive trees. Then the breeze stopped and Nana's sweet aroma filled the air around me.

"Nana are you here?" I whispered.

"Yes Jesus, I am here. I am always here with you."

I looked and, sure enough, there she was but this time she was all dressed in white and had a plume of feathers at her back. I fell to my knees and bowed my head in respect. I now knew her to be a messenger from God.

"Please stand Jesus. There is no need to kneel in front of me; it is you who is the son of God."

"Why me Nana? What right do I have to this title?"

"Your mother, Mary, was chosen to be the bearer of the saviour of humankind. Even though she was a virgin, she carried you in her womb. You were born into humble beginnings in a stable to avoid attracting any attention. You have lived your life as others do but with special knowledge. You have fulfilled the task set you and I am very pleased with you. But now it is time for you to take on the sin of the world. Now it is time for your final journey.

So, I tell you this. You will be betrayed by one of your disciples – the one they call Judas. He will sell you to the Romans for a bag of thirty silver coins. Peter too will denounce you three times as the cock crows.

Let these things happen and do not try to avoid them as they are inevitable and this is how it needs to be."

I was listening in sorrow and despair for I knew that my time would soon come to an end. To know it would be my friends who would cause this made me sad beyond belief.

"Do not worry about your friends. These actions are to help the future of humankind. You will have to be strong; stronger than you have ever been, in mind, body and soul. Have faith in me Jesus as I will be with you throughout it.

God will help you on your final journey and you shall be resurrected by God to serve your fellow man as the Holy Spirit. This will be your gift to all humankind so that they can live on through you and the Lord God Almighty."

This was a huge task for me to take on. How could I have the faith and strength to fulfil my destiny?

I paced back and forth with all sorts going through my mind. But if this was how it was meant to be then so be it. The choice had already been made for me. I braced myself and stood straight.

"I have lived a wonderful, fulfilling life. I have travelled to so many places, met and helped many people. I have been surrounded by my wonderful disciples, some of whom I now realise must betray me. This will be their destiny. To help save the future of humankind I will gladly give myself and bear no malice to those involved.

Thank you, Nana. You have always been there for me and I am ready for what the future holds for me."

There was a silence, one that seemed to last forever. I felt naked for I had bared all. The stillness of the night washed over me and I was calm, fulfilled and ready. Nana was there waiting like a marble statue, gleaming in the moonlight. The plumes wavered like a shiny spiderweb glistening.

"Are you ready my son?" she asked

"I am ready," I replied.

"Goodbye."

"Goodbye Nana."

I didn't know what to think or do but came to realise that my mission was coming to an end.

I looked out over the garden with all its splendour and stared down at my sleeping, unaware disciples. I sat down against the rock and drifted off to sleep.

We decided to venture back into the city. This time it was a safe journey and nobody bothered us.

We were a close-knit group and got on well together but what Nana had told me now made me feel slightly uneasy. I had accepted my fate but it wasn't real yet. I thought about Judas and what Nana had told me made me realise that he had changed.

He was elected as the caretaker of our finances and took charge of our meagre purse strings. Any money that we collected along the way, that was either given or we had earned through our skills, went into that purse.

Unfortunately, Judas could not resist temptation and every now and then he would use some for his own pleasure without asking. We all knew about it and as long as he didn't go too far we had accepted what he was doing. He was never questioned when money went missing. Did he know that we knew? Only he could tell us and he chose not to talk about it.

Despite the coffers being low, I had decided that we should go to a local tavern where I would deliver my news over a meal. It had been a while since we had tasted the good wine at the wedding in Cana and we could do with a good feed.

That night we made our way to the Mount of Zion where there was an excellent tavern. This was ideally situated outside the walls of Jerusalem so that we didn't have to encounter any Roman guards. We made our way along the goat path towards the tavern and we were in high spirits, laughing and telling stories. Peter walked alongside me as my companion.

"This is a good idea Jesus. I think we all could do with some light relief."

I looked at him and smiled.

"What?" he asked.

"Nothing my friend. It will indeed be a welcome change."

We arrived at the tavern and made our way to the back room which had been laid out for us. There was a long table that overlooked the valley, down through the olive groves and up to Jerusalem. Each took their place at the table and I ended up in the middle, passing plates left and right. It was a veritable feast and wine flowed nicely till all were filled.

The time came for me to make my announcement. I wasn't looking forward to this as it had been such a pleasant evening. I was nervous and my palms began to sweat. I had always tried to give help or comfort with my words. This time, my words would be devastating. Nevertheless, I could not let that stop me; I had to say them.

I banged my cup on the table to get everyone's attention – they were a real rabble. I sighed and began to speak.

"Thank you all for your support over the years. We have seen many things and have been to many places. Today I have called you here for a special reason."

I looked around at their expectant, puzzled faces. This is it. The time of destiny.

"My friends. I have to tell you about my prophecy. Within the year… I will die."

There was a deathly silence and thunderstruck faces. Then mayhem.

"No! Please Master, no," they screamed.

There was agony in their faces. None could believe my words. This had hit them like a bolt from hell. I tried to calm them and carried on.

"It has been foretold that one of you will betray me and this shall be my end."

Again, my words, like daggers, slowly pierced them.

"One of you will deny me three times before the cock crows in the morning."

They all stood up and pleaded their denial that they could never betray me. I tried to calm them.

"Do not worry. For these things that you will do are right. They are foretold. They need to happen and your actions will help fulfil the prophecy. Then, when the time comes, I shall rise to be at the right hand of my father."

I couldn't help but feel sorry for my companions. One minute they were happy, enjoying good food, wine and laughter and the next, distraught. I had to carry on though, hard as it was. Strange as it seemed, my feelings at first were sickening but as I carried on, I found an inner strength that guided my words and brought peace to my delivery.

"I ask you all to take this bread, which is my body and eat. Then take this red wine, which is my blood and drink. Do this in remembrance of me."

I passed the bread and wine around and we all took it together. This seemed to calm them and as they received it, they sat back down.

"But fear not, there is good news. After three days, I shall rise up and be back with you all."

They looked at each other bemused. I could tell by their faces that this was hard to understand. Judas was first to speak.

"How can this be Master? Who amongst us will do these awful things?"

I looked him square into his eyes and whispered into his ear.

"Go Judas and do what you must do."

His expression contorted into a look of horror, with tears falling down his face. With no explanation, he stood and left. The others, unaware of this, were crying and trying to come to terms with my proclamation.

Peter came to me, "How can this be Master, for we all love you as our own?"

I took his hand and gave him the bad news.

"Unfortunately, it is you, Peter, who will deny me."

He sat down and put his head into his hands in disbelief. The news came like a lightning bolt. All were upset and deeply affected by what I had said.

Gradually we left and made our way back to camp. It was a sombre walk and not many spoke. All were deep in thought, wondering who amongst them would do these awful things. All hoped it wouldn't be them. The guilty had already been informed and the innocent were completely unaware.

We arrived back at Gethsemane and went to our favourite spot. Nobody spoke, for all were filled with dread. An hour passed and then another. Then we heard voices and saw torches flickering in the dark night. We all stood to see who was coming.

It was the Rabbis with Roman guards and Judas.

"Stay where you are and do not move," growled one of the guards.

"We have come for the false Messiah."

I stepped forward.

"On whose authority do you do this?"

The guard didn't like his authority to be questioned but replied, "In the name of Pontius Pilate, governor of Israel. Now, which one of you is it?"

A Rabbi looked at Judas expectantly.

"Come forward and earn your money."

Judas came out of the shadows and came up to me. His face was expressionless but his mouth quivered. He kissed me on my cheek, whispering an apology.

The other disciples gasped in horror at what they had witnessed.

"So it was Judas!" said one.

The Rabbi produced a small leather pouch which jingled as he threw it to Judas. Judas caught it as if it was red hot and looked at me shaking his head, then ran off into the night.

The Rabbi, pleased with his purchase, pointed a long bony finger at me.

"Arrest that man!" he commanded the guards.

A guard stepped forward to arrest me. My brother Simon stepped in with a knife and lashed out at the guard, badly slashing his ear.

"Simon, do not defend me. Stay back."

The guards rushed forward, pushing him over hitting him with clubs.

"STOP!" I cried. "I will come with you but you must leave my friends alone."

As the guard came nearer, I saw it was Malchus, the guard from Jerusalem where we met Matthew. I looked at his ear and it was bleeding very heavily. I put my hand on it and smiled. Malchus didn't flinch or make a sound; he just let me carry on as he knew it was right. This was to be my last mortal miracle. His ear healed.

"Thank you, Jesus and I am sorry for what I do. It is not my wish."

"I know Malchus. I am ready and I will come peacefully."

The mob, led by a very smug chief Rabbi, raised their torches and cheered as they led me away. They threatened the rest of the disciples as they went. Scared for their lives, they dispersed and ran into the dark.

Judas ran and when he could run no more, he sat panting on the ground.

"What have I done? I have betrayed the Lamb of God and for what? Thirty pieces of silver."

He opened the little red bag and the contents shined out at him. He quickly drew the string and clutched it in his hands, shouting out loud.

"Forgive me, Lord. I was weak and I didn't know what I was doing!"

He broke down and cried. Then he stopped as an idea formed in his head.

"I'll take the money back. That's what I'll do. I'll take it back and say I was wrong." He stuffed the bag into his coat and made his way back into Jerusalem to see the Rabbis.

Finding some in the synagogue, he immediately went to one of the elders and gave the coins back to him.

"Please take these back. I was wrong. I made a terrible mistake."

The Rabbi looked at him and emptied the coins onto the floor.

"If it's your mistake, you take care of it."

Smiling in triumph, they left Judas on his knees and walked out of the synagogue to join the procession.

He was found hanging from a tree two days later.

The guards led me through the city gates where masses of people were now gathering. Many of them were believers and shouted words of praise and support. Others had not been converted in the way of the Lord and were controlled by the Rabbis. They were scared to show any support so joined in jeering at me, calling me a blasphemer and a false prophet.

Some of my disciples had come to see what was happening but kept out of sight. I spotted Peter as he made the mistake of stepping out of a doorway. One of the crowd recognised him.

"Here is one! I know his face."

The crowd turned to look and were now working up to a frenzy.

Peter, scared for his life, yelled, "No, you are wrong! I don't know him."

Another shouted, "Yes you are. You are the one called Peter. You're his right-hand man "

Peter was frantic at this point.

"No, please. I'm not him. I do not know this man."

But the crowd persisted.

"I do not know him!"

They pushed him to the wall and left him so they could catch up with my procession.

Peter sat against the wall sobbing. Looking up, he realised that the sun was just coming up and he put his hands over his ears and sobbed as he heard a cockerel as it made its morning proclamation.

I was being led by the guard but was not bound or shackled. The Rabbis headed up the procession. The crowds parted in reverence in front of them. We were on our way to see the Roman leader Pontius Pilate, who I understood to be a reasonable man for a Roman. I was taken into the garrison and made to kneel on the floor in respect of him. It was a long wait and I became tired. Being on my knees was not easy but the guards were more than happy to give me a helpful prod with their spears. The big wooden doors opened and in strutted Pontius Pilate. He made himself comfortable on his ornate, cushioned chair.

"Stand up," he ordered.

After being so long on my knees, I found it hard.

"Why are you here?" he quizzed. "What have you done so wrong to have the Rabbis bring you here with an armed guard and an angry mob?"

He came down from his chair and stood in front of me.

He looked me up and down.

"I can find nothing physically wrong with you, so it must be something you have done or said. Are you the one who professes to be the Messiah?"

Once again, I was being asked this question.

"It's not me giving me this name – it's others."

I thought it best not to antagonise Pilate. He walked slowly around me, stroking his chin.

"So you're not the son of God then?"

"As I told the Rabbis, we are ALL the son of God, so therefore yes… yes I am."

He nodded, "Yes, I see what you are saying but that doesn't help matters. What with the incident with money lenders at the synagogue and the fact that you're telling everyone to convert to your way, you haven't done anything wrong?"

I was wondering where he was going with this.

"I have decided to keep you here. Not as a prisoner but for your own safety and I will have to decide what is to become of you."

He waved his hand and I was led away. Still not bound. Still not a prisoner but not free to leave either as I was put in an unlocked cell.

Over the next few days, the Rabbis began pressurising Pilate into taking action against me. They used the people as a weapon.

"If you do not get rid of this blasphemer, the people will think you soft and a bad ruler. You must get rid of him."

Pilate turned his head and brushed them away with his hand.

"Leave me. I must think about this and will give you my verdict tomorrow."

Pilate was finding it hard to condemn me as he knew that I had done nothing wrong in his eyes but had a duty to keep the peace with the Rabbis. They had great influence over the people. He loved this position that Rome had given him here in Jerusalem. It was an easy job and he never had any major problems. But this was different. This was a huge problem.

The next morning the Rabbis came to Pilate and see what he had decided. They waited for him and eventually he came into the room with two of his advisors. He was solemn as he sat in his chair of office.

"Welcome Rabbi. I have made my decision. On the next Passover, I will give the people the power over Jesus' life. They shall either shout for Jesus, who you say is a heretic or Barabbas who is a well-known murderer and a thief. Then whoever the people choose, I will pardon and release. Do you agree with this?"

The Rabbis discussed this proposal amongst themselves and agreed that this would be acceptable. Pilate clapped his hands, "Well, that's settled then. I'm happy with that. I shall see you again at Passover."

The day came and there was a big crowd in the square which was becoming agitated. Each person had their view as to who should be saved and they could not agree between them.

The Rabbis were determined that my fate should be certain and so had paid a group of men to cause trouble. When the time came, they were to shout out *Barabbas'* name.

Pilate came out onto his balcony to address the crowd.

"Today, as always at Passover, I give you, my people, the power of granting a pardon."

The crowd cheered and Pilate thanked them.

"This year, there are two candidates for you to choose from; Barabbas who is a known thief and murderer."

The crowd booed, except for those men supplied by the Rabbis.

"The other is Jesus of Nazareth who has been accused of blasphemy."

There were cheers and boos from the crowd.

"So my people, who is it to be? Barabbas or Jesus?"

The noise was so loud that he could not hear the words that people were saying so he raised his arms to calm them.

"If you want to pardon Barabbas shout out now."

The paid men held knives at the backs of the crowd to make them shout out.

"Or is it to be Jesus that you pardon?"

Once again, the paid men held their knives to the backs of those in front of them as a threat not to shout for me.

This time, the shouts for me were far less. My fate was sealed. I was sent to save humankind yet they could not save me.

Pilate quietened the crowd.

"Then by the will of the people, I release Barabbas." Pilate waved his hands in disgust; he felt uneasy at the decision the crowd had made.

The guards on the other hand were delighted and happily took me away but this time in chains. There was to be no civility now I was branded a criminal and one with a death sentence.

Pilate wanted no part in the proceedings as in his heart he still couldn't justify my arrest. Even with all power granted from Rome, it was nothing compared to the Rabbis and the people. His face said it all as I was led away.

The Roman guards now made it very clear that I was to be mocked and ridiculed as much as possible. As they pushed me onto the cell floor, one of them spat at me.

"Where is your God now, Jew?"

They all laughed. As they left, each one left an imprint of his boot in my ribs. This time the door was locked.

This was it. It had begun. With a cough of blood, I went to my knees, clasped my hands and closed my eyes.

"Oh heavenly Father. Give me the strength to get through this. I know that I must endure pain and suffering so that humankind will not. I know that I must die to take away the sins of the world. If I falter, please do not think any less of me. I will try not to be weak so that this will not be in vain. Soon I shall be with you in heaven."

Then, a small beam of light shone through the bars of my cell window. As it landed on the floor in front of me, I put the palms of my hands into the light and I knew then that soon I would be taking my last breath.

Not long later, two guards unlocked the door and burst in demanding that I stand. One grabbed my shirt, pulled me out and pushed me forward. I did not resist or complain as there was no point. I knew my fate and now I had come to terms with it. God would be with me.

"Move, King of the Jews. We've got a little present for you."

He pushed me into a room that had a large tree trunk in the middle of it. Two large iron chains were hanging from it, with the stains of the last poor unfortunate wretch still shining in the candlelight.

They grabbed my hands, took off my shackles and put

them into the clasps attached to the chains. My clothing
was ripped from my back.

"Brace yourself, Jew."

He lashed into me with a whip with leather tails. My
skin ripped savagely with every stroke.

After ten strokes the other guard took over and he let
fly with the whip. As both were standing there out of
breath, a third guard appeared.

"Here, King of the Jews, I have made
you a crown. Every King should have
a crown."

He held a circle of thorns in
his hand and proudly showed
his friends what he had made,
taunting them with the thorns.
Then he turned to face me. I
was hanging from my shackles
with blood running from my
open wounds.

"I crown thee King of the
Jews."

With a swish of his hand, he
forced the thorns onto my head and
pushed them into my skin. Blood
spurted from where the thorns dug
into me and dribbled into my eyes.
I was floating as if on water. The sounds of the guards
drifted in and out of my head. I couldn't understand their
voices as they were like the whooshes of the desert wind.

Another guard appeared.

"Bring him up. Pilate wants him upstairs," he barked.

They unshackled my bleeding hands and dragged me onto my bruised feet.

"You heard him. Pilate wants to see you. Ain't you lucky."

And with a dig in the ribs, I was forced to walk up the steps to where Pilate was pacing the floor.

"Bring him to the balcony," he ordered.

I was shuffled through a room to a balcony where Pilate addressed the public. I left blood trails along the nice clean marble floor. Pilate came onto the balcony and addressed the crowd.

"I have tried but can still find no fault with this man. What shall become of him?"

One of the Rabbi's men stood forward.

"Crucify him! Nail him up," he shouted.

All his supporters clapped and cheered. They didn't even know who I was. Pilate looked around the crowd with a feeling of helplessness.

"Then I have no choice but to grant the wishes of the people. He will be crucified."

The cries of many were drowned out by the cheers of the few. Pilate turned to me.

"This is not of my doing. I act on behalf of the people for the people. Please forgive me."

I stood there swaying on my weak, battered legs and whispered through my spilt lips, "As you have repented, you will be forgiven."

He searched my face, bowed his head and waved his arm.

I was dragged out and taken through the back doors into the courtyard where a group of soldiers were waiting. On the floor was a big wooden cross. My bleeding feet carried me across the soft sand towards the waiting soldiers.

"Is this him? Not what I expected," one remarked.

He bent down and picked up the cross.

"Here King, this looks about your size."

He dropped the wooden cross onto my shoulder. It dug into the wounds left from the lashing and my legs faltered under the pain but I managed somehow to stay standing.

"Come on then we're going for a walk," he jeered and whipped me like a donkey on my other side to make me start walking.

Slowly and painfully, I started my journey through the city's long thin passages. My legs gave way under the pain and the weight of the cross, and I fell. Again, I was donkey whipped. I managed to keep my balance and got up. I carried on, almost floating, unable to feel my feet.

There were people along the way, some crying when they saw me, others jeering. I could hear no one. All I could hear was the sound of wind in my head.

Then, all of a sudden, a woman was standing in front of me screaming something, with tears rolling down her face. I managed to stop for a second to look at her. Her face was familiar but my eyes were swollen and bloody and I couldn't quite make out her features.

Then I heard her words.

"My son. My beautiful son. What are they doing to you?"

It was my mother. How could this be?

"Lord, please don't let her see me like this."

Another lady came over to her, pitied her and helped her to one side. I looked at the lady and she knew. The whip cracked again; there was no mercy. On I went but my legs, although floating, were giving in and as much as that whip cracked, I could not go on.

A soldier, seeing this, told the others to halt.

He shouted to a man in the crowd. The man looked at the soldier, he was scared, like a rabbit in a trap.

"Come here and carry this cross," the soldier ordered.

At first, the man refused but the soldier cracked his whip at him and he came forward. I stared up at him.

"What is your name, friend?" I managed to whisper.

Startled the man looked at me and said "Simon... My name is Simon of Cyrene. Are you the one?"

I dribbled some blood from my lip and managed to say, "Yes I am he. And I bless you Simon of Cyrene."

With this, Simon picked up the cross and began to walk with it, with me beside him. No sooner had I started when my legs failed. And the whip came again.

"How much more Lord? Can this body take much more? I am finished."

My mind was in a bad place. My thoughts fuzzy. Then, once again, the shaft of light came down through the clouds and touched the floor in front of me. It gave me strength.

"Thank you, Lord."

I scrambled up and took the cross from Simon and walked slowly onwards. The crowd was still a deafening hum in my head, the people's faces unrepentant. I was today's entertainment, so I struggled on.

At the end of the road was a clearing where a group of soldiers was waiting. Women were crying and shouting my name. I could see my poor mother was one of them. I could do or say nothing now, so I let my feet carry me onwards towards the soldiers.

One of them grabbed the cross and laid it down on the ground, while others ripped off my clothing, leaving me with just a loincloth. I fell to my knees, now too weak to stand and the soldiers lifted me towards the cross. They dropped me onto it and splinters dug into my flesh. I winced, for the pain was unmeasurable.

A soldier grabbed my arm and placed my hand on the right side of the cross, aimed a long sharp iron nail at my wrist, paused, looked at me, smiled and drove the nail in with three big whacks of his hammer. I tried to scream but could not. He did the same to my other wrist. I floated. Then came the final nail. Two soldiers held my feet together while the third placed the iron spike at my feet.

There was no remorse. This was his job. I was not the first and I would not be the last. Then.

Wham…

Wham…

Wham.

I was secured to the cross. The pain was excruciating and I couldn't help but scream out.

There were three holes dug for the crosses to be placed at the top of the hill. It was decided that I would be placed in the middle. It was the highest point and everyone in the gathering crowds would be able to see the spectacle.

They dragged me alongside the middle hole, lifted me up, pointed my feet at the well-used hole in the rock and dropped me in with a thud. There I was hanging from a cross, not yet dead but slowly, oh so slowly dying.

A soldier came over to look up at me. He had a faint look of sympathy on his face.

"I know your story and that all you have done is good. I cannot bear to think of you suffering for days."

Then he took his long spear and pushed it sharply into my side. I looked down as he pierced my side. I understood his actions but still cried out.

"I do this to help you on your way. I will pray for you."

Either side of me were two men, also hanging from their crosses.

One said, "I am a thief, cheat and a liar. I deserve to be here. Why have they put you here? You don't deserve; you have done nothing wrong."

I can barely open my right eye.

Pain now immense.

But through this eye, I can see their faces. They are staring in disbelief.

"Forgive them Lord. For they know not what they do."

THE BEGINNING